The View from Enmore Road

THE VIEW FROM ENMORE ROAD

DORI MACLEAN

Selkirk
STORIES

ISBN 978-1-926494-38-8

Stories copyright © 2021 by Dori MacLean

Cover Photo copyright © 2021 by Dori MacLean

Author Photo copyright © 2021 by Heckbert Studios

Selkirk Stories™ and the image of a heart with three stars
are trademarks of Selkirk Stories, Cornwall,
Prince Edward Island, Canada.

Table of Contents

INTRODUCTION

I grew up on a small farm in Springhill, PEI, in the 1950's and 60's.

I was the eighth child in a family of nine and the last one at home after all my siblings had moved away for careers or marriage or both. That time alone with my parents gave me the opportunity to learn more about their younger lives.

They both grew up on the Enmore Road—with just the MacLaurin farm separating the Enman farm, my mother's home, from the Frost farm where my father grew up. They were friends from the time they were young children. In fact, my mother told me that she fell in love with my father when she was eight years old.

For as long as I can remember, I have loved hearing stories of past times. Stories about what life was like during my parent's childhood were always my favourites. I was fascinated by the varied personalities of the neighbours on the Enmore Road and by the struggles and joys of day-to-day life of my grandparents and great-grandparents.

Now that I have adult children, who have given me that greatest of gifts—grandchildren—I want to ensure that these stories are not forgotten. So I have recorded them here for all the generations of the Enman and Frost families who may follow … and for anyone else who likes to immerse themselves in stories of a time long gone.

A WALK IN THE WOODS

It was a great evening for cutting hay on the marsh. Tom Frost was whistling "Annie Laurie" as he strolled through the back fields with the sun on his shoulders and the salt wind in his hair. He had time now to do the work he enjoyed most since Alf had taken over the responsibility of farming. With his scythe over his shoulder he might have looked like the Grim Reaper, if he had been able to keep the smile off his face. Cutting marsh hay on Seal Point was one of his favourite chores. There was no big tear to get it done as the hay from the fields was already in the barn, enough to feed the animals for the winter. Marsh hay was just an extra treat for the horses, who loved the salt taste of it. Tom understood that right well as he, too, loved anything that smacked of the shore.

Just now his mind was strolling back through time to Sunday afternoons when he and Margaret would take the youngsters down to the shore for a picnic. They'd all go wading and perhaps they'd find enough quahaugs for supper. The two boys would paddle around in the old dory and the girls would tuck their skirts up and look for shells to use as doll dishes. He and Margaret would sit on the bank and sing all the old hymns together. She had had a sweet voice, Margaret. Tom had been brought up Baptist and it wouldn't do to be singing anything but hymns on a Sunday. Mind you, they sang the ballads from the old country together on Saturday nights when the work was done and the little girls wanted a song to put them to sleep. His whistle tune changed to

"The Bonny, Bonny Banks o' Loch Lomond," as the memories crowded his mind.

The sun was starting its slow slide down the western sky to the water as Tom arrived at the marsh. He began to swing the scythe in the steady rhythm that he could keep going for hours. He'd been doing this for years and his shoulder muscles no longer screamed with the effort as they had when he was a boy, trying to keep up with his father. Tom had been one of ten children, eight girls and two boys. His father had made his living as a postmaster, but everybody had to grow enough hay to feed their driving horses. You couldn't get by in the country without a few animals for the table, so there had been a pig and chickens for eggs and for eating. And of course, a garden big enough to keep the large family fed and some to preserve for the winter. Tom had learned enough working on his father's few acres to know that he wanted a real farm of his own some day. Now here he was, a contented man, cutting marsh hay on his own farmland at Seal Point in Enmore.

Tom worked up a good sweat and laid down a lot of hay before he looked up to realize that the sun, which had been dropping lower and lower, was now dipping into the water. He'd better be getting home before dark. He'd go home through the woods. It would already be dusk among the trees, but it was a shorter walk than through the fields and there was a good path.

He was strolling along, enjoying the cool breeze blowing up from the shore. Suddenly he saw a figure ahead of him, some distance up the path. He couldn't imagine who would be walking to the shore through the woods at this time of the evening. Must be one of his neighbours, though. Tom called out a greeting, expecting to hear a familiar voice in return. To his surprise there was no response at all. Now that was strange! Anybody in Enmore would know his voice and he couldn't think of a soul who wouldn't answer. The figure just continued walking toward him at a slow shuffle. It was quite dark here among the trees, so he couldn't get a good look to tell him who it was. The size and shape of the approaching figure didn't look at all familiar. Tom repeated his greeting and was quite annoyed when he still didn't get a response. The distance between them was getting shorter and Tom expected to recognize the person soon. Who did he know who was that tall and had that kind of shuffle when he walked? And why would one of his neighbours be taking the shore path with night coming on?

Just then he got a greeting all right! A loud "WHUFF," and Tom suddenly realized he'd been walking directly toward a black bear. The bear was walking upright on his hind legs. Without time for thought,

Tom let out an awful roar, swung the scythe off his shoulder toward the bear's head and jumped aside. The bear dropped to all fours and lumbered down the path past him as fast as it could go. It was soon out of sight around a bend. Tom was shaking! He sat down under a tree to catch his breath, wondering just how far along the path that bear had gone. He didn't like the idea of turning his back on the direction the bear had taken, but there was no other way home and he certainly didn't want to spend the night in the woods. Nothing to do but keep going. Off he started as fast as he could walk, keeping a tight hold on the handle of the scythe. Sometimes he felt like he was being watched or as if there was something coming up behind him, getting closer and closer. Once he was sure he heard breathing just over his shoulder. When he finally reached the last of the woods, with his shore fields in sight, he began to run.

He made it home just as the last of the light was leaving the sky. Collapsing on the cellar hatch, Tom took in great gulps of air. After he had sat there for awhile in the blue-dark, his chest heaving, he began to think of how big that bear had been. Must have been a foot over his head at least! And the shoulders on it nearly filled the width of the path. Its paws must have been three times the size of a man's hand. And the teeth! Good thing I swung that scythe when I did. If he'd have made a lunge at me I'd have had a hard time escaping those claws and teeth. Probably had never been another bear the size of that one seen on Prince Edward Island in years. The more he thought about it, the bigger that bear got!

Well sir! Wouldn't this be a story to tell at the ice cream social at the Victoria West Hall tomorrow night. Will MacLaurin would have quite the time trying to top this one!

MEAT HASH OR FISH HASH?

"What happened your leg, Tom?" asked Philip, stepping into the cosy little kitchen where Tom had lived alone since Margaret's death. Philip was always amazed at how tidy the house was kept. Not another man he knew would be able to keep house as neatly as Tom Frost did. Margaret would be smiling in heaven to know he was doing so well. Philip dropped in often because he knew how lonely Tom was without her and how long the days must be for him with no one to listen to his stories. He had also discovered that it was not a bad idea to drop in at mealtime. Tom was a good cook.

Philip sat himself down in the biggest rocking chair

and got comfortable as Tom limped around the stove putting the kettle on for a cup of tea. He knew there'd be a story about that limp and he knew he would hear it all in great detail if he just sat back and waited. Tom had a reputation for his tidiness and his ability as a cook, but mostly he had a reputation for his long-winded stories. Well, Philip had all the time in the world and he enjoyed a good yarn.

Tom was peeling potatoes and getting a frying pan ready, so Philip knew he was in for a good dinner. Handing him a cup of tea, Tom sat down in the other rocking chair while the potatoes sizzled in the pan. The smell of roasting pork from the oven reminded Philip's stomach that he'd been smart to drop in at this particular time of day.

For awhile they talked about how late the spring had been and how Alf's cattle had fared out over the winter. These two were old men now, but they never lost interest in how the farms were doing or how good the fishing was. They had spent their youth working from sun-up till sundown, trying to grow enough to keep their families fed. Some winters they had had to go to the lumber woods in Maine or New Brunswick to make enough money to keep body and soul together. It had been hard on the women, doing all the barn work with just the youngsters to help. In winter all but one of the cows would be dry, but that one would have to be milked. The children needed milk for their porridge. There would still be the feeding and bedding up to do, and shovelling out the manure. The wood would have to be split and carried in to keep the stoves going, night and day. Margaret and Philip's Mary, with the help of their children, had managed it all. There were lots more women like them in Enmore those years, keeping the home place going while their men were working in the lumber woods. It might have been the ordinary thing, but Tom and Philip were right proud of Margaret and Mary, just the same.

The two old men's weathered faces told the story of long days outside in the sun and the wind, plowing and planting and bringing in the crops. You'd never hear them complain about that. They'd been proud of their ability to work hard and grateful to have been blessed with strong backs and strong arms. They would not have traded their lives for anything different. There had been some hard times but they had never felt real want. For them, living on their own farms in Enmore, surrounded by family and friends, was the best life of all.

"So," Philip finally asked, "Are you going to tell me what happened to that leg?"

"Well now, I think it was last Wednesday … no, no, it must have been Thursday. No, Wednesday. It had to be Wednesday because that's the day I always see the Ladners hitching up the wagon to drive to Tyne Valley to sell eggs. I don't know how they ever get any eggs in that wagon, there's so many youngsters to take with them. You'd think surely the older girls would be able to stay home with the little ones, but I suppose a trip to Tyne Valley is something they wouldn't want to miss. They'd be all excited to see what's new in the millinery shop."

"So, you fell off the front step and hurt your leg?" Philip broke in, thinking he might be there till dark if this story didn't get going. He was determined that he wouldn't go home until he found out what happened.

"No, no, I wasn't outside when I was lookin' at the Ladners," Tom growled.

"So you fell downstairs!" says Philip. "Shouldna been spyin' on your neighbours, anyway. Serves you right!"

"I wasn't upstairs lookin' out the window," Tom

said. "I was makin' dinner and I heard a lot of noise, so I looked out the window right here to see what was goin' on. Those young ones of Ladners are a noisy bunch."

"You been livin' alone too long," Philip mumbled, "Should try livin' at my place if you want to hear noise.."Like most households in Enmore, there were three generations living under Philip's roof. There were times when Philip felt that escaping to Tom's quiet little house just might save his sanity.

"Any road," said Tom, ignoring him, "that's how I know it was Wednesday. And like I said, I was makin' dinner. I can't remember what I was makin'. It must have been something I needed patatas for because I had to get some out of the cellar."

Philip squirmed in his chair a little, but Tom didn't notice and he didn't get to the point of his story any faster. Tom shook his head, "I can't remember for the life of me if I was makin' meat hash or fish hash, but anyway just as I got to the top step of the cellar stairs I tripped and fell down cellar."

"Well what difference did it make what you were making for dinner, Tom? What made you fall down cellar?"

"Well now, I can't rightly remember that either! Musta caught my foot in somethin' on the top step. I wasn't thinkin' what I was doin', wonderin' how all those little Ladner youngsters were goin' to get in that truck wagon. Can't imagine how they'd get to Tyne Valley without one or two fallin' off."

"And that's how you hurt your leg? Lucky you didn't break it! Shouldn't be livin' here all by yourself. One of these days I'm gonna come in here and find you at the bottom of them cellar steps with yer head cracked open, that's what!"

Philip was sorry the minute the words were out of

his mouth because Tom started all over again at the beginning, trying to remember if he'd been making meat hash or fish hash and what it was that made him fall down cellar. "I might have known better than to start him off again," Philip said to himself, shaking his head. "Tom's stories have no shortcuts! I might have to get up and get a plate of dinner for meself!"

GRANDFATHER TOM

"Sit still, sit still," he said, as he came shuffling across the floor heading for his favourite chair. Lloyd, Alf and Christy's youngest, was curled up in it. Tom slept late in the mornings now. There was no reason for him to get up early any more. His lack of usefulness on the farm was hard on his pride. He had had to finally admit to himself that his arthritic old frame would no longer do the work that had been required of it for so many years. He was just a burden to his children now, or so he thought.

His Margaret had been gone for a few years now. Called to her final reward the minister said. Tom knew it would be a good one. If anyone deserved a place in heaven, Margaret did. Memories of their life together were what kept him going these days. He would never forget the day they were married, April 14, 1877. You wouldn't have seen a prettier bride anywhere. No other woman he had ever known had had a smile like hers. Tom had been a bit of a ladies' man until he met Margaret. His friends said he would never settle down. It sure surprised them when he courted Margaret for months before she agreed to marry him. She kept insisting that he should find someone closer to his own age. He had known there was no one else for him, from that first walk home from church in the moonlight. She was twenty-nine the day they wed and he only twenty-four. She wasn't the only one to think she was too old for him. Most women had three or four children by the time they were her age. Tom wasn't worried about that. They soon had four fine children, two boys and two girls.

Life had been good to them.

Alf was the youngest boy, so of course he inherited the farm when Tom got too old to look after things anymore. It was the old tradition on Prince Edward Island that the youngest boy got the farm—whether he wanted it or not, some said. Along with the farm came the responsibility of looking after the parents in their sunset years.

Tom hadn't had a farm handed down to him. His father wasn't much of a farmer. John Frost had been postmaster in O'Leary when Tom was growing up. Of course everybody had to have a barn for their driving horses and hay and oats had to be grown to feed them. Tom had enjoyed looking after the horses and the milk cow. He liked feeding the chickens, too. He guessed he had always known that he wanted a real farm of his own some day. When he married Margaret, he had to find his own bit of land and clear enough of it to grow his crops and pasture his animals. Margaret had worked right alongside him, burning the stumps when the trees were cut and plowing around them until they were rotted enough to be pulled out of the ground by the team. They were long days and short nights in those early years, but they had done it all together. It had been a good life.

The only thing that gave him heartache was that Margaret had left him too soon. They had had thirty-two years together. Oh, how he wished it could have been longer. The children had grown up and gone to the States to work, as he had done himself as a young man. Rob and Eva had both married and made their lives there. Alf was the only one who had returned to Enmore. Anna had eventually gone to Alberta, where she married and raised her family. Margaret had not been here to grieve with him when Rob was killed by a streetcar at the age of forty-two or when Anna's husband had died so young, leaving her with the children to bring up alone. Here he was, an old man and he still missed Margaret so much.

Alf and Christy had a fine family and he was grateful for his place in it, but he hadn't minded living alone. He could cook well enough for himself and he was a tidy man, so he had lived on his own quite awhile after Margaret's death. When his eyesight began to fail, Alf and Christy had insisted he move in with them. He didn't want them worrying or feeling they had to be checking on him all the time, so he finally agreed to give up the home he and Margaret had shared. He enjoyed having the young ones around, but he suspected they thought him a terrible old grouch. He took pride in the fact that the oldest grandson, Charles Thomas, had his name in reverse. He was Thomas Charles and had always been called Tom. Charlie reminded him of himself as a young man … a mind of his own and a spirit of adventure about him.

Charlie would be off to the States in the fall. His two older sisters, Marjorie and Jessie, had been living there for some time now. Jessie's husband was looking for someone to help him run his garage, so Charlie would have a job to get him started. Tom hoped Charlie would come back to the Island some day. He had a feeling that second daughter of Toff Enman's might bring him back. Yes, he was an old man but he could still recognize romance when he saw it.

Marjorie was encouraging Eva to go to Prince of Wales College in the fall to get a stenographer's course. She was even offering to pay Eva's tuition. There wasn't much work for young women on the Island, even less than for young men. For a man, it helped if you had a trade, or a farm to take over when the old ones were ready to let go. For a young woman in the country, teaching was about the only option other than marriage. Lots of girls were eager to get married and start a family right away, but Alf and Christy's daughters all seemed to have that same sense of adventure that Tom admired so much in Charlie. The two oldest were gone and he expected Eva and Anna to follow eventually. Lloyd was just a young lad yet, but no doubt Alf would be hoping he would take over the farm when the time came.

Ah well, he'd been staring out the window and letting his mind run long enough. But what else was he good for these days? And there was Lloyd, still sitting in his chair. They all knew that when he said "Sit still," he really meant "I want my chair now … " Lloyd waited till the very last minute, till Tom was one step away from sitting down. All the while chuckling inside, Tom had a hard time keeping the frown fixed on his face as Lloyd finally slipped off the chair. Hmm, perhaps this youngest one was going to be as much of a rascal as his older brother.

THE RACE

It's never easy growing old. When you've spent your whole life running a farm, providing for your family by long hours of hard work, old age might make you wonder if all that toil was worth the effort. However, if you have someone to continue what you've started, a son to build for the future with dreams of his own, it's easier to accept the aches and pains that old age brings. The greatest joy of all is to have grandchildren to fill your remaining years with love and pride.

Old Grandfather, with his long white whiskers and piercing blue eyes, was Theophilus Enman. He was called Offie by all who knew him. Offie had spent most of his seventy-three years as a farmer and he continued to think of himself that way although his son, Toff, was now in charge of the farm. Even as he grew too old to handle much of the farm work, he wanted to make himself useful in any way that he could. He liked to go to the barn to help with the milking, morning and evening. This was more of a problem than a help to Toff and Liza, but they would never have thought of refusing him. That would have been a terrible blow to his pride.

At the ages of five and six Toff and Liza's girls, Annie and May, were given their own chores around the farm. They would gather the eggs, make sure the barn kittens got a saucer of milk and the old collie got his evening feed of scraps from the table. Sometimes they would even hold the bucket to feed the smallest calves.

One summer evening, Old Grandfather had milked the two quietest cows, as usual. He was not very steady on his feet any more, but he had a pail of milk in each hand which he was carrying to the house. Lumbering along on his bandy legs, trying to keep the milk pails from spilling over, he met the girls coming out of the hen house with their egg baskets full. Old Grandfather said to the girls in his raspy voice, "Bet I can race you to the house, without spilling a drop of milk." The girls looked at the tottery old man, looked at the very full milk pails, looked at one another—and giggled. "No you can't, Old Grandfather," Annie declared. "Startin' now," he said, and took off at a snail's pace with his doddering two-foot shuffle.

The girls thought this would be just too easy. They got a good grip on their baskets—they knew that they didn't dare break those eggs—and started a fast walk behind him. Watching his skinny bow legs jigging back and forth was just too much for them. Just as they were about to get past him they broke into a fit of giggles, which soon became gales of laughter. They laughed so hard that they had to sit right down in the middle of the path so their eggs wouldn't fall out and get smashed. With tears of laughter stream-ing down their faces, they watched Old Grandfather slowly, slowly make his way up to the house. When he reached the doorstep he turned around to look at the two little girls, who were rolling in the grass laughing. With a twinkle in his eye he announced, "Told you I could race you!"

OLD GRANDFATHER AND THE BULL

In Old Grandfather's time, a man's worth was tied to his ability to do a day's work and do it well. This was out of necessity, of course, but it was also a matter of pride. On Prince Edward Island when there was just a farmer and his horses with no motor-driven machinery, it was hard work from early morning until the sun went down. Spring, summer, fall and even in winter, with the crops safely stored and the animals in the barn, there was plenty of work to be done. The animals must be fed and watered, their stalls kept clean and dry. Old Grandfather, like most small landholders of his time, was a "terrible hard worker."

There was lots of woodland that needed to be cut down to make more room for planting, so when the crops were in, Old Grandfather would go to clearing land. The trees would be useful as firewood, but the stumps would need to be burned where they were. For a few years after the clearing was done they would have to harrow around the stumps and plant between them until they would be rotted enough so that the land could be levelled out by the plow. It was hard labour clearing land with just a sharp axe and the strength of your arms, but it was work that needed to be done. Late fall was the best time of the year to do it. Offie would choose a woodlot close to pasture land and get down to business.

One fall day when the rhythm of swinging the axe and connecting with the tree was feeling particularly fine, Offie was startled by the sound of a cranky old bull bellowing and snorting in the pasture next to him. The great black beast was tearing up and down the fence line between the pasture and the woodlot, pawing up clods of earth, challenging to battle this intruder in his domain. Offie ignored this display of ownership — until he heard the fence posts break!

There was no time to think. Offie found himself scrambling up the nearest hardwood that had limbs low enough to hold onto, axe still in hand. He got onto a crotch in the tree, flung one leg over and dared not climb any higher. The bull, who had just reached the bottom of the tree, was working himself into a fury. He was smashing that trunk with his massive head. Fortunately the tree was a sturdy old maple, but its branches were shaking with each blow. Offie realized that the sun would soon be going down on this short autumn day. Would he have to spend the night in the tree with an angry bull trying to shake him out of it? Would he be able to hang on while the bull did his best to knock him to the ground? He no longer had the strength of a young man and he had never felt less sure of himself.

Forethought can be lost in the panic of the moment. Offie wrapped his legs tighter around his branch, grasped the axe handle in both hands and swung the blunt side of the axe head with as much force as he could muster. At that moment the bull was about to batter the tree one more time. Good fortune was riding on Offie's shoulders. His blow with the blunt of the axehead connected, just between the bull's horns. The beast staggered backwards, shook his head and let out a monstrous roar!

Offie braced himself against the tree trunk, his eyes closed tightly. He waited. He felt nothing. When he dared to open his eyes, he watched with amazement as the bull went stumbling off through the hole in the fence. The great beast was shaking his head and staggering his way to the back of the pasture, as far from Offie's tree as he could possibly get.

Offie was a long time holding on to the limb with his shaky old legs before the sun went down below the trees. Finally, seeing and hearing nothing more of his opponent, and with every bit of his body feeling as if it was made of water, he dropped the axe and slowly eased himself down out of that old maple and began the long walk home through the woods.

Just before he got to the farmyard, he met May and Annie coming to look for him. Running to him, they called out in frightened voices, "Old Grandfather, where were you? We were so worried about you. Mama and Papa were worried too. We heard a bull roaring. Did the bull scare you, Old Grandfather?"

"Oh, girls," he said, "I have quite a story to tell you tonight! But first, I think I'll just have a drink of water, and a bite to eat."

When he had had something to eat, Old Grandfather dropped wearily into his rocking chair and closed his eyes. He was almost asleep when he opened them to find himself looking into two eager, worried little faces. May and Annie were staring intently at him from their place at his feet. "Girls," he asked, in his ragged old voice, "Did you ever imagine that your old grandfather can still climb a tree?"

OLD GRANDFATHER AND THE HORSES

If a farmer didn't like horses—if he was afraid of them, didn't trust them, or treated them harshly—farm work would be a constant battle. Horses who were well cared for, fed and watered regularly and provided with a clean stall after a hard day's work, were a great asset to a farm. To get the best from horses, they need to be treated with respect and kindness. They need to be in top physical condition, never abused with overwork or ill-treatment. A farmer who was careful of his horses was usually successful in all aspects of farming. Offie Enman, Old Grandfather, was just such a farmer.

Old Grandfather loved his horses. There were no tractors in Offie Enman's time, so he and his strong, sturdy horses had to do the work of farming together. The horses hauled the wood sleigh to get out the yearly firewood; they pulled the potato digger, the hay-cutter, the manure spreader, the plow. Even Sunday was not a day of rest for the horses. That was the day to take the family to church and to visit neighbours.

As Offie's steps grew slower, his eyesight dimmer, his body weaker, he refused to give up the care of his beloved horses. He was still the one to feed them, keep their stalls clean and bedded with fresh straw, even when he could no longer work in the fields and the woods along with them.

In every season but winter, when they weren't needed for farm labour, the horses were pastured close to the house. Offie liked to watch them from the fence rail while they cropped the grass with their strong teeth, drank from the brook that ran through the pasture, ran with their tails streaming behind them in the wind, or just lay down under the maples to rest. He was the one who checked their hooves for stones, the one who made sure to pitch new hay into the pasture when the grass was getting cropped too close. When you've spent your whole life as a farmer, from the time you were a boy, you find ways to make yourself useful even when there is much you can no longer do.

One fall day Grandfather was left home alone with May and Annie while Toff and Liza went to Tyne Valley for groceries. The girls were playing contentedly with their dolls in the house. Old Grandfather went for a slow walk around the farm buildings, checking on things. As always, he ended up at the fence rail to watch the horses. Suddenly the girls heard him shouting! "Annie, May, come quick, help me get the gate shut! The horses will get out!" The girls ran to the window and there was Old Grandfather, desperately trying to latch the gate while the horses came thundering from the far end of the pasture. Somehow the gate had been left only partly latched. Discovering this, Old Grandfather was frantically trying to get it fastened tightly. The horses, seeing Old Grandfather at the gate, probably thought he had apples for them as he so often did. To make matters worse, in his haste to get the gate securely closed before the horses discovered it open, Old Grandfather had gotten his long white whiskers tangled in the gate latch!

"Girls!" He was roaring now, "Come out and help me! I'm caught! Can't you see I'm caught! The horses will get out! Come help me!" What the girls saw was Old Grandfather dancing around like a leprechaun, yanking on his long beard and only snagging it tighter for his efforts. It was an hilarious sight. The girls may have been of some help to Old Grandfather if they hadn't been laughing so hard they could barely walk, let alone run, to his aid. He reminded the two little girls of Rumplestiltskin, as he jumped and stomped and tugged at his whiskers. Before the girls reached him, the great work horses clomped through the open gate, down the lane and onto the road, heading to North Enmore.

When Mama and Papa arrived, just minutes after the horse's escape, the girls were desperately trying to untangle Old Grandfather from the gate latch. The poor old man was humiliated to think that he hadn't been able to prevent his beloved horses from getting away. However it wasn't long before Mama and Papa, with help from the MacLaurin's, caught up with the horses who were stopping to graze by the roadside. They headed them back home and got them safely into their own pasture, with the gate latched tightly behind them.

Old Grandfather never quite forgave the girls for laughing at him. But for years after, whenever things got too quiet or dull around the Enman house, Annie would only have to look at May and say "Rumplestiltskin," and the two of them would break into a fit of giggles, remembering.

FILL MY PITCHER

Old Grandfather grew weary with age. He could no longer do much on the farm, except to walk to the barn to see that his horses were being well cared for. He spent his winter days sitting in his rocking chair by the stove where he and Old Grandmother would watch the world go by on the Enmore Road.

Unfortunately for everyone else in the house, they filled their days arguing about everyone who passed by their window. If a young Ladner from down the road drove by with his horse and sleigh, Old Grandfather might say, "There goes Joe's youngest boy. I hear he's turning out to be a right smart young fella. Great help to his father." Old Grandmother would snap at him, "That's never Joe's youngest. They must have at least two younger than him." And the duel was on! They could spend a whole morning trying to convince each other which of Joe Ladner's sons was the youngest. After dinner, they would start all over again when someone else went by. It might be how long a couple had been married, how many children they had, or who their parents were that would be reason enough for disagreement. In fact their whole lineage, right back to the old country, could be fodder for a rousing discussion. It seemed they made a point of never agreeing on anything. Old Grandmother had a sharp tongue at the best of times, but Old Grandfather seemed to revel in getting her riled up.

After Johanna's death in February of 1915, Old Grandfather's health began a serious decline. Perhaps those arguments had given him something to look forward to every day. He fell ill with what was called at the time 'a wasting sickness'. He was constantly thirsty and drank copious amounts of water which "ran right through him." He could no longer do anything for himself and had to stay in bed, day and night, in a downstairs bedroom as he could no longer climb the stairs. It became the job of little May to be sure Old Grandfather always had water in the pitcher on his bedside table. He would call out to her in his deep, harsh old voice "May, May, come fill up my pitcher." May would drop whatever she was doing and run to his room to get the pitcher from his table, pump it full of water, pour him a cupful and help him take a drink. She didn't realize that he was dying, but she loved Old Grandfather and she wanted to do whatever she could to help him. On a good day, she would sit with him awhile and he would tell her stories about his life as a young man. He could always make her laugh, telling of scrapes he got himself into.

His death came on Oct. 13, 1917. May was not yet ten, Annie was eleven. Sid, their little brother, was nearly four.

The children were, no doubt, shielded from the sight of Old Grandfather's body being carried out to be embalmed and returned home in a casket. The wake was at the farmhouse, as all wakes were in those times. The girls would, no doubt, have been told to sit quietly in the kitchen entertaining their little brother. Mama and Papa would need to be in the parlour to meet the neighbours who filed quietly past the casket to pay their respects to the family of this well-loved man. The quiet lingered in the house for many days following the funeral.

About a week after the funeral, May was asked to stay at home to keep the fire going while Toff, Liza and Annie went to the field to pick potatoes. It was a warm, sunny autumn day, so they took Sid with them. May was sitting outside on the old stone doorstep, when suddenly she heard, as clear as could be, that dear old raspy voice. "May, May, come fill up my pitcher!" She was up and running to the pump, pitcher in her hand, before she stopped herself. But she had heard him. He had called her.

She had tried not to make a fuss at the funeral. She told herself she would not "take on." Old Grandfather would not have wanted that. Even in her bed at night she had just sobbed quietly into her pillow, not wanting to upset anyone with her grief. But here alone in the kitchen where she had filled his pitcher so many times, she cried her child's heart out for the grandfather she had loved so much.

Many, many years later, when she was coming to old age herself, she told me that she believed that you got to meet people again in heaven that you had loved on earth. She said she hoped it was so, for she wished

with all her heart to see Old Grandfather again.

THREE COFFINS

Old tales from Celtic folklore are often told in circles of three—three sons, three gifts, three tasks to be accomplished. The Scots who emigrated to Prince Edward Island carried those stories across the ocean with them. Their folklore was part of their essence, helping to define who they were. Norman MacLennan was a Scots-Canadian who believed deeply in the old tales of his ancestors. He saw omens in the world around him and was very aware of the significance of the supernatural in his life.

As this story begins, Norman MacLennan is operating a successful sawmill on Trout River in Victoria West. The people of Victoria West and all the surrounding communities rely on Norman to saw their lumber when they need to build a house, a barn, a boat, or even a pig pen. It is Norman they come to when a new baby is in need of a cradle or when a loved one passes away and a coffin is required. The sawmill is essential to the day-to-day life of his neighbours and Norman is proud of his ability to serve his community well.

The problem for Norman is that, like most other businesses in the area, the sawmill he operates is not his own. It is owned by James Yeo, the ship-building magnate of Port Hill. It sticks in Norman's craw that with his skill and his long hours of labour he makes money for James Yeo, instead of for himself. He receives only the wage Mr. Yeo is willing to pay him for his services. He has offered to buy the mill, of course, but Mr. Yeo will have none of that. James Yeo hasn't become the richest man on Prince Edward

Island by selling anything that is making him money. So each time Norman asks, Mr. Yeo refuses and Norman's frustration grows.

Norman never allows that frustration to impede his work. It is his nature to be the best sawyer he can be, no matter who reaps the profits. Whatever the task asked of him, he does it to the best of his ability. He keeps the mill as tidy as he possibly can, given the nature of the milling business. When a job is finished, the mill is swept out and the sawdust removed before he begins the next job. His tools are sharp and clean and always kept in their proper place, so that he wastes no time looking for anything. Sometimes his neighbours chuckle behind his back that he is "as fussy as an old housewife." Norman doesn't care what they think. As long as he is the one operating the mill, he will run it his way. He doesn't mind the neighbours hanging around, waiting for him to finish a job for them, as long as they stay out of his way and let him get on with his work. If they don't, he isn't shy about letting them know it. They're willing to put up with his crankiness because they respect his workmanship.

Norman has never left the nightly closing of the mill to anyone else. It is his job and his alone. Every evening when the day's work is done and his helper gone home, Norman goes through the mill checking all the working parts, making sure everything is in shipshape for the next day's sawing. He stops the huge waterwheel, makes sure all the saws are sharp and the mill tidy. Only when all this is done will he go home to his supper and his night's rest.

One evening in the fall of the year as Norman walked up the hill to his home overlooking the stream he took note of the darkening sky. "Storm coming," he thought, "To be expected this time of year." The family had just finished supper when the rain began, beating on the roof of the old farmhouse like nails being driven by a hammer. "A good night to be tucked into your own bed, with a roof that doesn't leak," said Norman. Knowing his roof was tight, he was soon sound asleep under Sophie's warm quilts.

Sometime in the wee hours, Norman was jolted out of sleep by a noise that was not part of the storm. He sat up and listened, not believing his ears. Through the rain and the wind he could hear it. He was sure only one thing could be making that sound. The sawmill gear was running! He jumped out of bed, pulling on his pants as he stood up. In minutes he was rushing down the hill to the sawmill in the pouring rain. As he ran he was trying to imagine how this could have happened. He knew he had stopped the wheel before he left the mill. He did that every night, and he could clearly remember doing it tonight. So how could the mill be running now?

He stood for a moment at the door of the mill and listened. Perhaps it was the sound of the wild wind roaring through the trees that he was hearing. No, it was not his imagination. The mill was running. He pulled the door open quickly, half expecting to see some youngsters climbing out the back windows. The minute he opened the door, the noise stopped. The machinery was still. But he had heard it! The sound of the mill running was like the sound of his own breathing, it was so familiar to him. How could it be that he had heard the mill running all the way from the house and now that he was inside the mill that sound was gone? No one could have got the wheel stopped that quickly, especially not youngsters playing a trick. Carefully, Norman searched the entire mill, looking for a clue to solve this mystery. He found nothing. Not one piece of wood was out of place. Everything was just the same as when he had closed the mill down and gone in for supper. Norman stood for a long time inside the quiet mill, his eyes searching everywhere, trying to make sense of this. Finally he opened the door and walked slowly back up the hill to the house in the pouring rain. He stripped off his wet clothes, hung them to dry by the wood stove, and went on up to bed.

Norman was sure he would get no rest this night, but the effect of the long day's work soon took over and he dropped into a deep sleep. He was dreaming, dreaming he could hear the sawmill running. Suddenly he was wide awake again. He could hear the sawmill running! Surely it couldn't be. But it was. Once more he was out into the wild wind and rain, down the hill to the mill. This time he didn't hesitate. He flung the door open, searching every corner with his sharp eyes. Nothing. No sound, no movement. The mill was as quiet as it had been when he shut it down at supper time. But he had heard it. He had heard it all the way down the path from the house, as clearly as he had heard it when it woke him. Were there young fellows playing a trick on him? Surely no one would be out on a night like this playing tricks. Was he losing his mind? Once more he made a good search. When he still found no answers, he started walking slowly up the hill, paying no attention to the cold rain running down his neck.

Back under the warm quilts, he tried to reason out what might be happening. Soon exhaustion took over, however, and he was drifting into sleep again. He was just on the edge, just about to fall into the depths of forgetfulness, when he was jerked wide awake for the third time. Again he could hear it! The mill was running. Norman MacLennan was descended from a long line of Celtic ancestors. Belief in the spirit world ran strong in his Scottish blood. Until now he had been looking for a physical explanation for what was happening, but it became clear to him at this moment that this was no ordinary experience. Something or someone beyond human understanding was at work in his sawmill.

The practical side of his nature demanded that he check the mill again, just in case. In the pouring rain he rushed down the hill once more. This time it wasn't just the rain that was sending cold ripples down his spine. Of course, when he opened the door the mill was just as he'd left it. Just as he had left it two other times tonight. He shuddered at the thought of turning his back on the mill to go up the hill to the house.

When he went inside this time he poked up the fire and hung his dripping coat behind the stove. He put the kettle on to boil for a cup of tea. Sophie heard him and she was soon sitting beside him at the kitchen table, listening to him tell about the night he'd spent.

"There must be a message in it somewhere," Norman said. "Something I'm supposed to do or know about." His head hung down; he looked beaten. He was a practical man who always faced his problems head on, but this was a problem he had no way to solve.

He and Sophie sat there in silence, each lost in their own thoughts, trying to find some sense in the strangeness of this night. The rain had stopped. Dawn was beginning to break across the eastern sky, sending its fingers of light into the quiet kitchen. They were drowsy with interrupted sleep, the hot tea, and the warmth of the fire. The disrupted sleep had left them exhausted and their eyelids were drooping. Suddenly, there was a knock on the door. They looked at one another, startled. No neighbour would knock. They would just call out and step inside. Could this night become any more uncanny?

When Norman called out, "Come in," the man who

stepped inside was not familiar. "Norman MacLennan," he said, without a word of greeting, "I'm the captain of the Mary Jean. We were blown off course last night in the storm. We ran aground and were smashed to pieces by the waves. We lost three of the crew. The folk who helped us get the bodies out of the water told us that you're the one who makes the coffins around here. Would you be kind enough to make three coffins so we can give our sailors a Christian burial?"

Three coffins. Three times the sawmill machinery had started in the night. The legends of his homeland had come to haunt him.

Not long after that stormy night, Norman MacLennan decided to carry out a plan that had been in his mind for some time. He would leave Prince Edward Island and join his son, Isaac, in British Columbia. Packing up his tools and his family, Norman crossed the country, leaving the sawmill on the Trout River to Mr. Yeo. He found work as a sawyer in the booming lumber industry of the west coast, where the money he earned was his own. With a new life in a new place, he truly hoped he had left his ghosts far behind him.

DOWN AT THE SHORE

Old Grandfather said that if you were born close to the water you had salt in your blood and you were never happy too far from the shore. In Enmore, as you lay in bed on a windy night in the fall, you could hear the waves crashing on the shore. The roar of the breakers would call you to come down and dance in the sand with that wild wind. In a winter storm the grinding of the ice could wake you from your dreams. On a spring day you could feel the salt spray in the air, taste it on your tongue. Summer, however, was the sweetest season on this little island in the Gulf of Saint Lawrence. In summer the onshore winds could blow as softly and sweetly as tropical breezes.

A child could wile away the day making roads in the sand, digging holes with quahaug shells, running in and out of the water to get cooled off.

One spring, Alf Frost built a sailboat at Frost's Creek with help from Toff Enman. It was a flat-bottomed boat, about eighteen feet long with a centre board and a rudder for steering. Most Enmore families had a dory, as fishing was a sideline to farming. Nearly everybody fished to add a bit of extra cash. They also fished because, as Old Grandfather said, the saltwater was in your blood when you lived that close to the shore. Being in a boat was almost as natural as walking to the Enmore people. Children learned to row a dory as soon as they were big enough to handle the oars.

About the middle of June was quahaug fishing time. The crops would be in the ground, each seed getting ready to sprout. While they waited for the crops to grow ready for harvesting, everybody who had a dory would go down to the water at low tide and pick quahaugs to sell. Some dories had a sail and some just oars. The littlest children would climb in over the side before the boat was in deep water and stake out their place at the back so they wouldn't be left behind. If they grew impatient waiting for the grown-ups, they could always rock the boat to see if they could knock each other out.

Sometimes everybody would go to Mossy Point, sometimes to Little Island or the Sand Bar. The whole family, often three generations, would work away together feeling the quahaugs with their feet, trying to see who could find the biggest ones. The mothers would pack a lunch so it was a big picnic when all the neighbours stopped to eat together on the shore. This was the part the littlest ones liked best—having all their friends together without having to go to school.

At Portage Shore, Wallace Noye had a float where

he measured what each family had picked. He would pack the quahaugs in ice and by evening they would be on their way to Boston or the Fulton Fish Market in New York City.

Sometimes on the way home from fishing, the boats loaded with quahaugs and families would race to the Portage shore to see who could be the first to sell their quahaugs. Charlie remembered one time when his father's boat, carrying six people, got caught out in a gale and had a hard time getting to shore. The winds were so strong that the sail kept swinging from side to side and dipping into the water. Everybody in the boat was kept busy ducking so that they wouldn't be knocked overboard. Alf kept the sail up as long as possible so there would be less distance to row the heavy load. The people watching from the shore were very afraid the boat wasn't going to make it. The people in the boat were almost certain they wouldn't make it! Only one or two of them knew how to swim and it would have taken a strong swimmer to fight those waves. What a relief to finally reach shore and stand on dry land again! They really earned the money they got for their quahaugs that day.

When they finally drifted off to sleep that night the wind was still howling around the eaves and rain was pounding on their windows. No doubt there were many grateful prayers sent to the gates of heaven for the lives spared that day from death in the water.

About October, after the harvest, was oyster fishing time. Alf Frost and Will MacLaurin would leave Sunday evening with a horse and buggy and drive the fifteen miles to Grand River to fish oysters. Alf would board with a cousin's family for the week. When he got home on Saturday night Christy and the children were eager to hear the stories he would have to tell. They were full of questions about what the weather was like, how many barrels of oysters he fished, what he did if there were days too stormy to fish. Alf always had funny tales of things that happened while they were on the water. Once he dropped his tongs over the side of the boat and as he was reaching for them he almost bumped heads with a seal who had poked his head above water, as if wondering what in the world those things were.

The children liked hearing about his oyster fishing time, but were excited to have him back, as their life didn't seem quite right when he was not at home with them.

In spring, perhaps early in May, Alf would put a net out in the bay for about a week to get enough herring for the family. One small barrel of salt herring was all the family would use, so if he got more than that he would give away what he didn't need. They were tasty fried up for supper. The Frost children thought nobody could fry herring nearly as well as their mother.

The farm and the shore had many life lessons to offer the children who grew up there. Those lessons, along with the example of their parents, helped them become confident, responsible adults.

BRINGING THE COWS HOME

"Do I have to go for the cows tonight? Can't Rob go with Alf?" Anna was only eight years old and she didn't like the long walk down the back lane to bring the cows home for milking. Alf was twelve but their mother didn't want him to go alone in case the cows were hard to find. She didn't often send Anna as she knew it was quite a walk for her short legs, but tonight Rob was busy helping their father and there was no one but Anna to go with Alf.

They had walked nearly half a mile through the fields and into the woods before they heard the bell-cow's bell ringing. The other cows would be with her, they knew. Usually the cows wandered home by milking time, but not this evening. It was still early fall, but the days were getting shorter and dark seemed to come earlier in the woods. Why, oh why, did those darn cows have to be in the woods tonight?

The children could hear the cow bell, but they still didn't see the cows. If they didn't find the cows soon, they were afraid they might get lost in the woods. Anna was determined not to let Alf see her cry, but it was all she could do to keep the tears from coming. The woods were getting darker and darker as the sun sank and they got farther from the back fields of the farm. They kept walking, staying close together. Alf wouldn't admit it, but he didn't like being in the woods after dark any more than Anna.

The sun had gone down and it was blue-dark now, but the bell-cow sounded nearer. Suddenly there she was just ahead of them. They called out and ran toward her but she turned and walked away from them when they got close. That's when they heard the roll of thunder. That explained it. The cows had sensed the storm coming and felt safer in the woods. There they were, the whole herd, lying down among the trees. Alf and Anna tried to get them up but they wouldn't budge. Even though their udders were full and they wanted to be milked, they were afraid to leave the woods.

Now it was really getting dark and Alf wasn't sure he could find his way out of the woods at night, with so little light left in the sky. There was a fallen tree beside the cows and Alf and Anna were tired from their long walk. "Let's sit down here and have a rest, Anna. Maybe the thunder will stop in a bit and we can persuade the cows to come home then." So the two children sat close together on the log near the cows because they really didn't know what else to do. Then the rain came down, pelting the two children like little stones until they were soon soaked. They knew they would get lost for sure now if they tried to find their way home in the dark woods, which went on and on behind the Enmore farms. They felt safest huddled there with the cows.

Back at the farm, Tom and Margaret started to worry when it began to get dark and the children didn't come back with the cows. Tom realized that the cows must be too afraid of the coming storm to leave the shelter of the woods. He got a lantern and started toward the woods where he thought the cows might be. Margaret ran to the neighbours and soon there were more men with lanterns following Tom's light. They walked through the woods for a long time, calling the children's names, but Alf and Anna couldn't hear them over the noise of the wild wind and the rain. It was nearly ten o'clock before they found the two frightened children deep in the woods, drenched and shivering, huddled next to the cows for warmth.

When Anna saw the light coming through the woods and realized it was her father come to bring them home, she called out, "Oh Pop, I knew you'd come!" She had been so brave, but now that Pop was here she couldn't keep the tears back any longer. He picked her up in his strong arms and carried her home, with Alf walking close beside him. Tom knew he'd have to be up before daybreak to get the cows home, because they'd never follow him tonight through the storm.

When they got their wet clothes off and got into their warm beds, it wasn't long until the exhausted children fell fast asleep. Tom and Margaret lay awake long into the night, talking quietly together of how he might not have found them until morning if it hadn't been for neighbours so willing to go out into a cold, rainy night to help him search. "Good thing we live in Enmore!" Tom said, as his body finally began to

relax into sleep.

UNCLE MALCOLM

Every family has its characters—some who do the family reputation no good, some who are full of fun and mischief, and some who just march to the beat of their own drummer. Christy Frost's brother, Malcolm MacLeod, was one of those who, in his later years for sure, marched to his own drummer.

Malcolm was tall and lean. He had a bushy moustache and he smoked a pipe so constantly that it seemed almost a part of his face. He would never have been considered a handsome man, but the twinkle in his eyes and his mischievous grin were what folks noticed most about him.

He married Mary MacKenzie and moved away from Enmore to the Long River area. To his Enmore family It seemed like a world away, considering that the main means of travel were by horse and wagon or by train. He and Mary had three children—Flora, John Alex, and Annabelle. Not long after the youngest was born, Mary died at the age of thirty-three. Malcolm had little time for grief with three small children to care for on his own. When Mary's sister offered to take them in he realized that she could give them a better home than he could. They needed a mother and their aunt loved her sister's children dearly. The children grew up with their aunt and uncle, but they weren't far from their father's home and they were able to spend more time with him as they grew older.

By the time his children were grown and making lives of their own, Malcolm's life was beginning to be lonely. He decided to spend some time with his sister,

Christy, and her family in Enmore. He knew that his brother-in-law, Alf, was trying to get some more land cleared. Lloyd was too young to be of much help and Charlie had gone to the United States to make a living, so Malcolm offered to move to Enmore for awhile and help Alf with the farm work. They spent long days cutting trees, hauling them home to the farmyard, blocking them up for firewood. Morning and evening the cows had to be milked and the animals fed and watered. After the trees were cut, the stumps had to be burned so that the new field would be ready to plant grain, potatoes or buckwheat. Alf would have had a hard time getting it all done on his own and the hard work helped to ease Malcolm's lonely heart. He stayed for a few months with Christy's family, until after the planting in the spring.

Christy was happy to be able to help ease Malcolm's loneliness. Her children loved their Uncle Malcolm.

He was a quiet, gentle man with a sense of humour. He loved to tell stories of places he had been or people he had met as a young man, travelling around Canada and the United States. After the spring work was done, Malcolm would go back to his home in Long River so he could be near his children, but every year he returned to Enmore for a long visit. Christy would never know when he was coming, as he had no means of travelling except to hitch a ride with someone who was going west. They would look out the window some morning and see him wending his way up the lane and the children would go running to meet him.

By the time Alf and Christy's children were grown up and making their way in the world, Malcolm was living with his daughter, Annabelle, and her husband, Frank Brown. Alf's oldest son, Charlie, had married May Enman and they bought a little farm in Springhill and began filling the house with children. When the oldest children were grown and gone to homes of their own, Malcolm asked if he might buy a small cabin for himself and move it into Charlie's farmyard. Charlie and May were glad to have him do this. He lived there for a few seasons, from late spring to fall. He would have his main meal with the family, but he had a little stove to cook his own breakfast and supper. He always had ginger snaps that he bought at Reub Enman's store to give to the children when they stopped in to visit. His cabin was tiny, but he kept it neat and tidy, with a place for everything.

Malcolm rarely bothered to trim his bushy moustache and it became a source of fascination for May and Charlie's three youngest girls. When he ate meals with the family, the girls would watch with great amusement when he drank his tea. The bottom of that bushy moustache would become completely soaked in tea. The girls would look at one another and start to giggle, until Mum caught their eyes and quietly shook her head. Then it was all they could do to stifle the laughter until the meal was over and Malcolm went back to his own little cabin. The girls would go into gales of laughter doing imitations for one another of how Uncle Malcolm would be trying to get the tea washed out of his moustache.

After Malcolm moved back to Long River, he would visit Charlie and May just as he had visited Alf and Christy—arriving unannounced, by whatever means he could find to hitch a ride. He was getting up in years by this time, probably in his late sixties. One morning, as May was about to go out to hang clothes on the line, she heard a roaring noise which seemed to be getting louder and closer. It sounded a bit like a very low-flying airplane. When she looked out the window, there was a motorcycle flying down the lane with Uncle Malcolm hanging on to the driver for dear life, looking like he might be thrown into the ditch at any moment. The driver brought his motorcycle to an abrupt halt in a cloud of dust at the doorstep. Malcolm scrambled off, thanked the driver for the ride, and the motorcycle roared away again. Malcolm had nothing to say about his ride on the motorcycle, but he was happy to sit in the kitchen with a strong cup of tea for quite a while before he wandered out to the barn to find Charlie. He told Charlie that he thought that ride was probably what it would be like to be caught up in a whirlwind. You never knew when you might be thrown off or where in the world you might land. "I just hung onto him," he said. "If I flew off that thing, he was coming with me."

Later he told the family that he thought perhaps one ride on a motorcycle would be just about enough for him for this lifetime!

WILL AND MARY

Will MacLaurin was a yarn-spinner. There was no more welcome sight on the Enmore Road than to see Will come sauntering up your lane of a summer evening after the chores were done. He would often step into Alf and Christy's kitchen, settle himself into the offered rocking chair, and the tale-swapping would begin. The two youngest Frost girls, Eva and Anna, would curl up on the knees of the story-tellers. After an hour or so they would begin to get sleepy, listening to their father and Will tell the size of the fish they'd caught this summer or the wonderful horses they'd owned over the years. The girls especially liked the wild tales of their days in the lumber woods in Maine and New Brunswick. Some of these tales were not meant for little ears, so before the men forgot who was listening, Christy would trundle the girls off to bed. The yarns would go on into the wee hours of the morning, the girls listening from their beds until they were lulled to sleep by the squeak of the rocking chairs. Suddenly Will would look out the window and realize that somehow it had become pitch dark outside. He'd grab his cap and say, "Dear heavens, I'd better be gettin' home. It'll soon be time to go lookin' for the cows!"

Mary Enman, Offie and Johanna's second daughter, was Will's wife. Will and Mary had a family of seven sons and three daughters. They farmed the land between the Enman and Frost farms on Enmore Road. Toff Enman, Alf Frost, and Will were the best of friends, helping one another with planting and harvest and anything else that required an extra hand or team of horses.

Will loved hunting and fishing as much as he loved swapping tales. To be down at the shore with a gun in his hand and a dog by his side was his greatest pleasure. He could keep his family fed in summer with strings of fat trout from the brook and in the fall with geese and ducks from the shore. The trouble was that Will often forgot to mend the fences or finish the plowing while he was off hunting or fishing. The new-mown hay sometimes got rained on, and Will's potatoes were the last crop to be picked in Enmore. When Mary heard the cows bawling to be milked, out she would go to the barn muttering to herself, "Where is he now?" The boys learned to do farm chores early and the oldest girls looked after the littlest ones and kept house while their mother worked outside. Will often said that he was never cut out to be a farmer. He did the best he could, but for Will farming was drudgery.

Everybody liked Will. He was easy-going and full of fun. Both he and Mary were especially loved by May and Annie, Toff and Liza's little girls who lived next to the MacLaurin farm. They loved to run across the fields to Uncle Will and Aunt Mary's. If Mary was out hoeing her garden, she would quickly stuff her pipe into her apron pocket when she saw them coming. The girls would go into fits of giggling as they saw the smoke curling out of that pocket. Mary knew that the girls knew that she smoked the pipe, but she couldn't bring herself to actually let them see her smoke it. She wasn't proud of that habit, but habit it was and a hard one to break. She would send the girls into the kitchen for molasses cookies while she emptied the pipe to keep it from burning a hole in her apron.

Will and Mary's children were older than the Enman little ones so they enjoyed having the little girls come to visit. Will liked to show May and Annie where he'd found the fox den beside the hayfield or the robin's nest in the apple tree. Mary would let them stir the cookies she was mixing. Their older cousins were awfully good to them, too. May and Annie would be so excited when Charlie would let them go fishing with him. He would find them a spot on a log close to the brook and tell them to BE QUIET! One day he got a big fish on his hook and he got so excited he jumped on the end of their log and dumped both of them into the water. They thought it was an grand experience as they waded out, soaked and giggling. Charlie didn't think a bit of brook water would hurt them, but Mama was cross when she saw their pinafores all wet and covered with mud. She could never stay cross at Charlie for long, though. He could always make her laugh when she was trying to scold him.

Mary worked as hard as a man on the farm and growled at Will for not paying more attention to it.

Bob, the youngest son, had a lame leg. He had been playing in the brook one spring when he was just a lad and he got an infection. The doctor operated on his leg on the kitchen table and removed a piece of bone. No one in Enmore thought he would survive such an operation. Survive it he did, but he was left with a limp for the rest of his life.

One fall morning, Will went away. No one ever seemed to know what transpired between him and Mary. Did they have a row? There was much speculation among the neighbours about the reason for his leaving. Some felt it was a terrible thing Will did, leaving Mary with a farm to run and only Bob to help when the older boys went off to make a living elsewhere. Many of the Enmore men, however, understood how hard it would be to farm if you had no love for it. There was speculation that Will and Mary had agreed that he should go to find some kind of work he would like better than farming. No doubt he planned to send money back to them. Mary didn't tell anyone anything.

When Will didn't come back and they didn't hear from him, the older boys went looking for him. They thought he might have been killed in the Halifax Explosion, but they were not able to find his name among the records of the dead. Some of the neighbours thought that perhaps he might be working on a rum-runner off the coast of Nova Scotia. Perhaps he had gone north to the gold-fields. All of his sons' searching revealed nothing. Will MacLaurin, it seemed, had disappeared from the face of the earth.

The years passed and the older boys left the farm. The girls married and made lives of their own. Finally there was just Mary and Bob left. They kept on running the farm, just the two of them. Bob became a good farmer. It seemed that, unlike his father, he was happy farming. He married Vera and started his own family, and Mary loved each of the grandchildren dearly. She was happy to have the job of rocking them to sleep while Vera helped Bob do the farm work.

One day, many years later, May was home for the weekend from her teaching job in Bedeque. She was looking out the window toward Aunt Mary's house, when who did she see but Uncle Will coming across the fields to visit just as he had always done. She thought she was seeing a ghost! But it truly was Uncle Will, come back home again. She couldn't stop the tears of joy from spilling down her cheeks as she ran to meet him!

The story that went around Enmore was that when he walked in the door, Mary asked no questions. She just handed him his pipe and set his place at the table for supper.

It was easy to see that Will was not well. He sat in

his rocking chair and was glad to talk with anyone who came to visit, but there were no stories of where he had been, what he had been doing, or what he had seen of the larger world. If he told Mary of his life away, or what he had been doing for all those years, she never spoke of it to anyone. He was just contented to be in Enmore and Mary, it seemed, was contented to have him there.

Within three years of his return, Will MacLaurin was dead. Perhaps he had come home to die. The great American poet, Robert Frost, once wrote, "Home is the place where, when you have to go there, they have to take you in." That was surely a truth that both Will and Mary understood.

THE COURTSHIP OF TOFF AND LIZA

Liza MacLennan grew up knowing that she must to do everything as her father wished, just as her older sisters had done. Liza was a loving and obedient daughter. She understood what was expected of her and wanted to make her parents proud. She knew that sons were expected to follow their fathers in religion and in politics, but daughters were expected to follow their husbands. She also knew that her father felt very strongly about both religion and politics and would not take kindly to a suitor who did not share his views. None of this was a cause for concern to Liza, until she met Toff Enman.

Norman MacLennan, Liza's father, firmly believed

that he was meant to be in control of every aspect of his life. When he spoke, his family listened and were expected to obey. When Sophie cooked dinner, Norman would go to the stove and fill a plate for each of his nine children. He would expect each one to eat exactly what he gave them. He was not an unkind man, but he was certainly a man who intended to be always unquestionably in charge. Confidence in his skills as a sawyer and his ability to work hard made Norman the self-assured man he had become. He operated his sawmill with hard work and precision and he brought up his family in exactly the same way.

Norman's oldest children were growing to adulthood and leaving home. Isaac had already left Prince Edward Island heading for British Columbia to look for adventure and hopefully to find work in the lumbering trade. The two older girls, Maggie and Carrie, were married and settled down to lives of raising children and working beside their husbands on their farms. Liza was the oldest of the six still at home.

It was at a wedding shower in the Victoria West Hall that Liza and Toff became acquainted. Liza loved to dance and when her eyes met Toff's as they were "swinging" in the square dance, both of them knew that their world had shifted. She had grown up in Victoria West, he in Enmore. They lived only a few miles apart, but this was the first time they had met face-to-face. From that night at the dance, they looked for each other wherever they went. They were always hoping for a chance meeting, an opportunity to talk, if only for a few moments.

Toff Enman knew Norman MacLennan's reputation. He soon realized that Norman did not want Liza to have anything to do with him. He understood that Liza must respect her father's wishes but he wasn't sure of Norman's reason. He supposed it could have been religion. The Enmans were Methodist while the MacLennans were Presbyterian. Toff was aware that emotions ran high on matters both political and religious. It was, Toff realized, important to Norman to ensure that his daughters marry men of the same political stripe as himself and the same church affiliation. It could also be possible that the objection to Toff was because of Norman's ambition for Liza. He may have thought that the Enman farm, being so near the shore, was too marshy to provide a good living. Perhaps he wanted a finer place for Liza than what Toff was able to offer. Whatever his reasons, If her father saw Liza speaking to Toff at a community event, she was given the eye and she knew the conversation must end. She was forbidden to go riding with him in his wagon, even if there were other young people along. Norman was adamant that Liza was not to spend time with Toff Enman.

Somehow Liza and Toff did manage to meet, to talk, and to fall in love. Liza did not want to defy her father, but she soon realized that he was standing between her and the one who had become the centre of her world. They knew their courtship had to be a secret, at least until they could figure something out. Liza, knowing her father all too well, was not optimistic. Toff had no intention of letting her go. "We'll find a way, just be patient," he promised her.

The day came, as Norman's wife Sophie knew it would, when Norman was totally fed up with operating a sawmill to make money for James Yeo. He announced to his family that he had decided to pack up their belongings and join Isaac in British Columbia. Isaac's letters said there were wonderful opportunities there for someone with skills such as Norman possessed. It was also in the back of Norman's mind that it would be an exciting opportunity for Liza. He thought that surely such a fine-looking and pleasant young woman would find a young man in British Columbia who would meet her father's standards. She would soon forget this foolish notion she had about Toff Enman. Norman started making plans to begin a new life far away on the west coast of Canada, where the money he earned would be his own.

May 16, 1905, dawned clear and sunny. Norman and Sophie, with their six youngest children and their most important possessions packed into two wagons, began the long drive from Enmore to the train station in Summerside. Norman was in high spirits. He was sure that this would be a good move for his family. He also felt sure that Liza would be glad she had obediently come with them as soon as she met a man worthy to be her husband.

When they reached the train station, after the long ride from Enmore, everyone was glad to get down from the wagons to stretch their legs. Norman went inside to buy the tickets for the journey and to find a buyer for the horses and wagons. Sophie and the family were to water the horses and keep an eye on their belongings. They had plenty of time to walk around a bit before the train was due to leave.

While Norman was occupied inside, another wagon arrived at the station. It was driven by Toff Enman. As he and Liza had planned, he had brought his Uncle Joe and Aunt Mary to be witnesses to their marriage, which was about to take place. Liza, with her mother's blessing, drove with Toff to the nearby manse where the minister was waiting to perform the marriage ceremony. In a short time they stepped out into the sunshine as Mr. and Mrs. Theophilus Enman.

Back at the station Liza bravely faced her father with her new husband by her side. For once, Norman had very little to say. No point in raging after the deed was done. Sophie had a warm hug for her daughter and a loving wish for happiness for both of them. The younger sister and brothers, with wary side glances at their father, were all smiles as they congratulated the bride and groom.

Norman and Sophie lived in British Columbia for a few years. Their youngest daughter, Catherine Ann, married there. Neither she nor any of her brothers ever returned to live on Prince Edward Island. Norman did not make the fortune that he had hoped for in the West. He returned to Prince Edward Island for a short time, then he and Sophie packed up once more and tried the west again. By this time technology had changed the sawmill industry and the skills that had made Norman so successful at the mill on Trout River were no longer useful. He eventually returned to Prince Edward Island for good, a defeated, worn-out, sick old man, with his pride in tatters. Of the nine children who had grown up in the old house next to the sawmill, only three daughters were living on Prince Edward Island. The others had all sought their fortunes in western Canada.

Norman and Sophie had sold their home on their second trip west, so they had no place to live when they returned the second time. It was Toff and Liza who took them in and cared for them for the rest of their days. Perhaps Norman and Toff had made their peace long before, but I have often wondered how that proud old man felt, accepting the charity of the son-in-law he had once scorned as not good enough.

THAT'S WHAT IT IS TO HAVE CHILDREN

Winter was the best time for visiting. The fall work was all done and there was just the care of the animals to keep the men busy. The women were only too happy to set their chores aside and get away from home to have a chance to catch up on news with people they didn't see often. Visiting, especially to the homes of relatives, was an important part of Enmore life in those days. As soon as there was enough snow on the ground for the sleigh runners, the visits would begin.

Alf and Christy Frost had five children at this time. Lloyd was born a few years later. It was a lively household, the five all being close in age. When they went visiting, Alf would hitch the horse to the wood sleigh, put straw in the bottom and buffalo robes for the children to snuggle under. Off they would go, across the frozen river to the home of John and Mary Murray. They were a childless couple, cousins of Alf's, who lived in North Enmore. Alf and John had been good friends, growing up. John and Mary were a bit older than Alf and Christy but they always welcomed their visits, children and all. Before leaving home the children were given a warning: "Sit quietly and don't touch anything because the Murray's aren't used to little ones. And the cats aren't accustomed to children, so don't try to pet them."

Charlie was excited about the trip to North Enmore. He had just reached the age when he was longing to be allowed to drive the horses. As soon as he heard that the family was going visiting, he began trying to convince his father to let him drive.

"Pop, when we take the horse and sleigh over to Murray's today, can I drive Mike for a little while? Do you think I could, Pop? I'm strong enough now. I'll hold the reins tight and I won't let him run." Charlie was watching his father's face all the time he was making his plea. Sometimes his father would let him take the reins for awhile, if Mike was behaving and not too frisky. That made the whole trip worthwhile. Visiting older relatives, especially the Murray's who had nobody for him to play with, could be a long drawn-out day for a boy who didn't like to sit still.

When the horses had got over their first desire to run and had settled into a steady walk, Alf turned around to where Charlie was sitting at the back of the sleigh with his legs dangling over the side-boards. "Do you think you could keep them going steady now, Charlie?" Charlie's eyes lit up like stars. Pop was really going to let him drive the horses! Years later, when he was driving his own team on his own farm Charlie often remembered exactly how it felt to take the reins for the very first time.

Anna, the youngest girl, remembered one visit when she had paid careful attention to her mother's warning to all the children to be on their best behaviour. When they stepped into the house she had quickly sat down in the nearest chair. A screeching yowl was emitted from the chair and a cat went flying at a scrambling run! Mrs. Murray's sympathy was entirely for "poor Topsy!" Anna was mortified that she had gotten off to such a bad start. Topsy soon found a place to hide, but the other cats continued to yowl and hiss for the entire visit, if the children so much as looked at them.

Christy, like most women, was glad to put her endless chores aside for awhile. It was good to have the chance to sit and hear the news from around the community. She was interested to hear who had a new baby, or was expecting one; who was talking of marriage in the spring; if there had been any quilting frolics; and of course, there were always funny stories to relate about the community's characters. Enmore and North Enmore had their share of characters, who were always up to something to keep their neighbours laughing.

For the children, the highlight of a visit with older relatives was always the lunch. A lunch was always served, no matter the time of day. Mary's baking was famous. There was always tea, well diluted with milk for the children, and wonderful cookies, cake, and squares from Mary's kitchen. Not having children of her own to look after, she had time to do more elaborate baking than the young mothers in Enmore. Her cakes with their thick icing were famous and oh, the mouth-watering date squares!

It did seem a long afternoon for the children with nothing to do but listen to the adult conversation, but the lunch was every bit as delicious as they imagined it would be. Mary had given them wonderful picture books of faraway places to look at while the adults talked, so that had made the time go a bit more quickly.

Then it was back home across the river, with the moon lighting the way and the sleigh runners squeaking on the dry snow. Alf and Christy would sing old songs and hymns all the way home. It seemed to the children as if the stars were singing along. The youngest children would fall asleep, warm and cosy under the buffalo robes, with the swaying of the sleigh and the singing rocking them into dreamland.

At home, Alf would stop the horses at the door of the house and carry the sleeping ones inside. Christy would hurry them all into bed while he looked after the horses, as the fire in the wood stove would have died out while they were gone and the house would be getting cold.

Despite sometimes being scratched by the cats or burning their tongues on hot tea, the children liked these visits to the Murrays. They were a warm-hearted couple, very fond of Alf and Christy. Although they considered children a bit of a nuisance, they treated them kindly and looked forward to their visits.

In later years, Christy remembered that when the young Frosts were being rambunctious and had to be scolded, John Murray would shake his head and say "That's what it is to have children!" But when those children grew up and went to work, they would come home to visit in the summer bringing gifts. And when Christmas came, boxes of gifts would arrive in the mail. Then John Murray would say, in quite a different tone, "That's what it is to have children!"

A Woman's Work is Never Done

Down the centuries there has been a debate about who works hardest, a man or a woman. A family farm is one occupation that would seem to answer that question easily.

Farming in the earlier years of the twentieth century, before every farm had a tractor to pull farm machinery, was an occupation which required long hours of back-breaking labour. With only his horses to help him, a farmer worked from dawn to dusk. All of those long hours the farmer was either on his feet or on the seat of a piece of machinery, being jolted around violently while trying to control exactly where the horse and machine were going. He was out in all weathers—looking after animals, planting, harvesting, storing crops for the winter, cleaning stalls and pens and doing a hundred other tasks that are part of the work of running a farm. When his children were old enough they would be given tasks of varying difficulty to help with the never-ending work.

Surely the labour of farming would seem to be a way of life that would require much more intense work and longer hours from the farmer than that of the woman who ran the household and took care of the children. After all, hers was mostly indoor work.

Let's take a look at what the homemaker had to do. Her days were spent cooking on a wood stove which had to be fired up even on the hottest days of summer, sweeping and scrubbing and waxing the floors, washing clothing and bedding, baking bread and cookies, and taking care of the children from infancy until they were able to be trusted to be outside on their own. This does appear to be a shorter list, until one considers that a woman's work wasn't over when the sun went down. It was the mother who washed the dirty little faces and feet before they were tucked into bed. It was usually she who sang them a lullaby and fixed the cuts and bruises they had earned during their day's play. If one was sick, it was the mother who doctored them and rocked the sick one to sleep after the others had fallen into dreamland. If the baby cried in the night, if one of the children had a bad dream, if the covers came off and a little one was cold it was most often the mother who got up to comfort them until they could get to sleep again.

The mother rocked the cradle with one foot while scrubbing clothes on a washboard in a tub. It was also the homemaker's job to help milk the cows, wash the milk pails, separate the cream from the milk, churn the cream into butter. Sometimes she would have to take the little ones to the barn with her when she helped with the barn chores, especially at planting or harvest time when her husband was longer in the fields. Three hearty meals had to be prepared every day to give her husband the strength to get his work done and to keep her family healthy.

There was a story told about a neighbour who tried to "butter up" his wife when he needed extra help on the farm. When he had finished eating the wonderful meal she had prepared at noon, he said "Lovely, darlin,' lovely! Now, can you harrow in the stumps?" He was probably thinking that if he praised her cooking, then asked her to help while she was feeling flattered, she would be willing to do whatever was needed. Harrowing between the stumps of newly felled trees took strength and skill and was a time-consuming task, better suited to a man's strength than a woman's. Many a farm wife took on that task, though. It had to be done and the time for planting was only so long.

There were many chores which took a lot of the farm-wife's time, beyond taking care of her children and home and putting meals on the table. The wood stove had to be hot, even on the hottest summer days. Bread must be baked, meals must be cooked, water must be heated. It was usually the children's job to keep the woodbox full, but when they were too young for this task or when they were in school the mother would have to bring wood in from the shed when she needed it. Water had to be pumped to be sure the warming tank on the side of the stove was full so there would be warm water for washing clothes and dishes, scrubbing floors, and for washing hands and faces and dirty little feet in summer.

Most women made their own soap, as buying it was too expensive. Grease and fat would be saved and put in a large iron pot. After it was heated it was set in a cool place overnight. The next morning the layer of grease that had come to the top was skimmed off and put on the stove to warm. The other necessary ingredients, sugar, ammonia, borax, lye and water, would be added and stirred in. Older daughters could help with the stirring when they came home from school. With the stirring the soap would begin to form and come to the top of the pot. When it was "right" it would be poured into an enamel dishpan to cool and set. It would be cut into squares before it got too hard. If there was a large family it would be used up quickly for laundry as well as bathing and hand washing.

Mittens, socks, and sweaters must be knitted for all family members. After the sheep were sheared, the wool was washed and taken to the Woolen Mill to be made into skeins of yarn. When evening came, the farm wife would not be idle. As she sat in her rocking chair, her knitting needles would be busy making the mittens and socks her family needed to keep them warm.

Mats for the floor were necessary in the winter, as the wood stoves did little to keep the floors warm. These must be hooked by the woman of the house. Often they were made from strips of worn-out clothing and the farmer's wife would use a common pattern or design one of her own. The mat was tied into a large wooden frame, which took up a lot of space in a home filled with children. Sometimes neighbouring women would get together for a hooking frolic. It was work that needed to be done, but it became fun when a group of women sat down together to make a mat. The laughter and the chatting made the work go quickly and not seem like work at all. The women would go from house to house in the winter, while their children were in school, until each household had a new mat for their floor.

If a farm family had daughters, chores were taught to them as young as possible. Making butter was a chore that children could help with at quite a young age. First the milk would be strained and the cream saved. A barrel churn would hold about two or three milk pails of cream. A child could turn the handle on the barrel churn or push the plunger on an upright churn, but when one child felt as if her arms were falling off, another would need to take her place. After a while there would be a swishing sound, which meant that the butter was forming into lumps and the whey was sloshing around. Then "Mum" would be called and she would take over the last bit of churning until there were big soft lumps of butter. The mother would have to add the salt as she knew just how much was needed and how firm the butter should be. The butter was then put into a pan of cold water and kneaded with a butter paddle or by hand, changing the water often in order to get all the milk substance out. Next the water would be drained off and salt added if necessary. The helpers were rewarded with a glass of cold buttermilk with flecks of butter still in it. Children who grew up with homemade butter said that it was the best butter they ever tasted.

Laundry was another chore that girls could help with at quite a young age. In summer, as soon as they were tall enough, the girls could hang the clothes on the line to dry after they had been scrubbed in the tub on the scrub board. (This same tub would be washed out and used for baths.) Washing clothes was a once-a-week chore as it took most of a day to heat the water, scrub the clothes, rinse the soap out of them and hang them to dry. They would be hung outside, even in winter, as it was impossible to get all the water wrung out. When they were frozen stiff they would be brought inside to be hung as close to the wood stove as possible to finish drying. Then almost everything had to be ironed, as the materials used to make clothes would get very wrinkled. The irons were heated on top of the stove and when one lost its heat for pressing the clothes, it would be traded for a hot one.

While the girls were helping their mother, the boys were working with their father, cleaning out stalls, feeding hay and oats to the cows and horses, putting clean straw in the stalls. It was the children's job from a young age to feed the smaller livestock, such as hens and geese. The boys worked beside their father, learning from him how to do the tasks they would need to master if they were to become farmers. The girls worked beside their mother, learning how to look after a home.

So the question remains "Who worked the hardest,

man or woman?" Perhaps it's a question that has no answer. The farms … and the families … that were most successful, were the ones where everyone worked willingly together.

Have Some Prasarves, Toffy

Folks who lived along the Enmore Road were always willing to give one another a hand. This was the way of life in the countryside of Prince Edward Island. If someone's cows broke through their fence and had to be rounded up, if a wagon was stuck in the mud, if someone needed a ride to see the doctor or to visit a sick relative, there was always a neighbour to offer help. It was the very spirit of this small community. It would have been nothing less than shocking if an Enmore family had a problem of any kind without help arriving unasked, as soon as the neighbours were aware of the situation.

One particular kind of problem sometimes required

the men of the community to help one another. There weren't too many men in Enmore who didn't enjoy 'a little drink' once in a while. In fact, if a man stepped into his neighbour's barn when the work was finished on a Saturday evening, he would probably be disappointed if a bottle didn't appear from somewhere in the hay. Most Enmore women did not approve of their men keeping that bottle in the house. There may have even been a few women who weren't aware of its existence in the barn. A problem would only arise if someone were to get carried away with that particular enjoyment. If the situation became too much for the family to handle, a young messenger might be sent to a neighbour's house for a bit of help in getting things settled.

One autumn evening just such a messenger arrived at Toff Enman's door. "Mama asked if Toff could come and get Papa quieted down. He's makin' an awful mess." At the time of the messenger's arrival, Toff was just settling down to a great visit with his friend Harry. In the Enmore way of description, Harry was a man with 'neither a chick nor a child,' meaning that he had never married and had no family. Liza had just fed him a wonderful supper and he and Toff were settling down to a long chat. They started out by discussing politics, then on to cropping, farm animals, what they might expect for winter weather. Now they were getting down to the real purpose of the visit—the tall tales, many of which came out of their winters in the lumber woods.

When Liza explained what the young neighbour wanted, Toff apologized to Harry and said he'd be back soon. Harry decided he might be able to be of some help if he came along, so off the two of them went to see what could be done. They arrived to find that all of the family, except for the tipsy and tottering man of the house, were nowhere in sight. He was absolutely delighted to have company! He invited them into the kitchen and insisted they have a seat at the table where he was about to 'have a bite to eat.' They pulled chairs up to the table, thinking that getting some food into him might be just the thing.

As the table was being set, Harry and Toff wondered if every dish in that cupboard was about to meet its Nicodemus. There was a lot of unsure footwork going on from cupboard to table. Finally there were three places set, with a few extra forks and spoons, and only one teacup broken in the process. The host fell into his chair, barely making it without ending up on the floor. He went down sideways with a thump, grinning broadly at Toff and Harry. "Help yourself, help yourself," he said.

Toff and Harry were quite amused as there was no sign of anything to eat on the table, just empty plates.

The smile never left their host's face as he passed one empty plate after another, encouraging them to "eat up, there's lots more where this came from!" At one point he passed Toff a fancy little dish obviously intended to contain jam or jelly, urging "Have some 'prasarves,' Toffy!" There was nothing in the dish and even if there had been, there was no bread or biscuit to put it on. It was all Toff and Harry could do to keep from laughing out loud.

Staring deeply into Harry's eyes, their host asked very seriously, "And how's all your care, Harry?" Sober, he would have known all too well that Harry had no family depending on him. At this point, Harry and Toff could contain themselves no longer. This serious concern for all of Harry's nonexistent "care" got them laughing fit to split their sides. Thinking he had made a wonderful joke, their host joined in the laughter whole-heartedly.

By now their host's mood was greatly improved so the two friends suggested they might be getting along home, in case he was feeling like a bit of a rest. "No, no!" he said, "I'm doin' great!" But he was easily steered towards the kitchen couch, his eyes closing the minute he lay down. They made their escape, feeling quite sure he'd sleep for the rest of the evening.

Toff and Harry had a great laugh on their way home and for a time whenever and wherever the two of them met Toff would inquire with a very serious face, "How's all your care, Harry?"

THE GREAT WAR

"There's ashes falling out of the sky!" May ran into the house with her hair and her white pinafore covered in grey ash. She had gone outside without her coat on this early winter day to rescue her kitten because the dog was teasing it. She came rushing back inside immediately, her eyes round and full of fear. The date was December 6, 1917.

The next day the people of Enmore heard about the terrible collision in Halifax Harbour of the Imo and the Mont Blanc. The Mont Blanc was carrying explosives, enough to blow up much of the city. The ash continued to fall on Prince Edward Island for days, carried by the wind from the disaster area that was once the beautiful city of Halifax. There was no school in Enmore that week. Parents kept their children indoors for fear that they would inhale the falling ash. Farmers did as little outside work as possible, just going to the barn to milk their cows and keep their animals fed and watered. The horses and cows in their stalls, even the sheep and pigs in their pens, were uneasy and wild-eyed. This strange phenomenon made them nervous and restless. The idea of so many deaths and so much suffering sat heavily on the hearts of the Enmore folk, as they read about the devastation in the newspapers.

The ash that had settled on fields and buildings was finally blown away by the wind. Life returned to normal on the Enmore Road. At least it was as normal as could be possible with the world at war and many young men from Enmore far away, fighting to save the world from tyranny. At school the students worked at making kits to send to the children orphaned or injured by the Halifax disaster. They felt good to be doing something to help, as their parents did by sending candy, fruitcake and small necessities to the men at the Front. That 'war to end all wars' affected Enmore's children in many ways. Before the war they had not paid much attention to their parent's concerns. Now all the talk after church or at the store was about who had had news from their soldiers. Daily life, for children as well as adults, revolved around news of the war.

Growing up on the Enman family farm with a father who was the youngest of ten children and a mother who was the fourth of nine, the Enman children had a wealth of cousins. Many of them lived close by or just a wagon ride away. Several of the aunts and uncles, however, had moved to the United States when they grew up. Some of them had married there and made their lives far away from their Enmore home. Every year when summer came, the family visits would begin. It was a time for Toff's sisters and brothers to leave their wealthier lives in faraway cities and return to the simple farm where they had spent their childhood. Aunt Sophie, Toff's older sister, returned every summer.

Sophie's sons, Armand and Delbert, genuinely enjoyed their vacations on the farm. Although they were city boys and older than Annie and May, the cousins became close. The boys liked to help the girls gather eggs, shut the geese into their pen at night, feed the calves. May and Annie were happy that the boys were always so willing to give them a push on the apple-tree swing or play hide-and-seek with them. Many summer days the cousins spent climbing the maples by the brook or trying to tickle trout. Trout-tickling was a talent the American cousins never really mastered, although the Enmore boys all seemed able to do it so easily. You had to be able to lie perfectly still on your belly on the bank of the brook, put your hand into the cold water and wait. If you were lucky a trout would slide up next to the bank close to your hand. Moving your fingers very, very slowly you would slide them under the trout and flip him out of the water. Every day all summer the cousins tried to catch a fish this way, but they never got the hang of it. They enjoyed the freedom of the farm, however, where they could walk through the fields to the shore, take the dory out for a row or just roll up their pant legs and go wading on a hot summer day. When their visit was over, May and Annie were always sad to see them go, knowing it would be a whole year before they would see them again.

When the Great War broke out Delbert enlisted first. As soon as possible Armand joined him in uniform. The girls didn't understand why they found Mama crying in the pantry after hearing of their enlisting. Occasionally letters would come from their cousins in Europe, always upbeat, always positive. No mention to their farm family of the horrors they must have been seeing and experiencing. Although May and Annie were only seven and eight years old, they soon learned why Mama was so worried and they, too, waited anxiously for each letter to come.

One September day May was swinging on the apple-tree swing just at dusk. Perhaps she was thinking of her cousins so far away across the sea, fighting to keep the world free. A wind, a breath on her shoulder, made her turn and suddenly there was Armand beside her. He was dressed in his army uniform, standing with his hand on the swing-rope. She waited for him to speak, but he just looked at her and smiled. Then he was gone. She ran to the house to tell Mama. A terrible look came over Mama's face as if May had told her something very sad. May didn't understand. She was so happy to have seen Armand. For many days after, Mama ran to the mailbox the minute the mailman stopped. She would be quiet for a long time after she came up the lane. Finally, a letter came from Aunt Sophie, telling that she heard from the boys regularly and they were doing fine. Mama read it aloud to the girls. Sophie sent a picture of each of the boys in uniform. May said "Mama, that's what Armand was wearing when he came to push me on the swing. He looked just like this picture!" She had never seen a picture of him in uniform before.

Armand and Delbert both returned from that war uninjured. When May told this story many years later, I asked her what she thought it meant for Armand to come to her like that. She was quiet for awhile. Then she said that it made her happy. She said she never thought, as her mother must have, that it meant that Armand had been killed. "Perhaps," she said, "he knew how worried I was and he wanted to let me know that he was all right."

May was eleven years old when the First World War ended. Sadly, it was not the war to end all wars as the world had hoped. She was a young wife and mother when the Second World War began and this time she had to live with the fear of knowing her dear brother and many of her childhood friends had enlisted and gone overseas.

Maggie and May

"Hurry up, May! It's time for school and Maggie is waiting at the end of the lane."

The boys and girls of Enmore lived close enough to each other's homes to walk to school together and to play after school. The farmhouses faced the road and the fields spread out behind the barns down to the shore. The houses were usually quite large, as they were often built to be home to three generations living together. Families in Enmore numbered anywhere from two to fourteen in the early years of the 20th century. The family in which May Enman grew up was a very small one compared to most along the Enmore road, but there were three generations of

Enmans in the household. Her parents had both had many brothers and sisters and all of the grandparents and great-grandparents had had many siblings. Toff and Liza's family consisted of three children —Annie, May and Sid.

May had been a sickly baby, in fact she was not expected to live through her first year. She tottered on the brink between life and death for her first three months, and there were many setbacks until she reached her first birthday when she began to thrive and grow stronger. Her older sister, Annie, was healthy and strong and thus she was allowed to get out into Enmore's childhood society as soon as she started school. May was kept close to home so she could be watched carefully, as she remained small and thin and seemed very frail. She wasn't sent to school until she was almost seven, although she could have gone a year earlier.

Until Annie started school, the two sisters had been best friends. Annie made new friends at school and May resented the secrets she shared with them. She didn't like being left out. The summer before May started school Mama suggested that she could invite Maggie MacArthur, her next-door neighbour, over to play. Annie had been invited to play at a friend's house for the day, so May was delighted to have a friend to play with who was just her age. From that day, May and Maggie would spend long summer days under the Lombardy poplars in the lane playing with their dolls, preparing delicious mud pies decorated with daisies and dandelions, swinging on the rope-swing in the Enman yard or looking for kittens in the straw on the MacArthur barn floor. When Christmas came, May couldn't wait to run over to MacArthur's as soon as her presents were opened to share her excitement with Maggie.

May and Maggie walked to school together when August came, white pinnies over their dresses to keep them clean, their soft light-brown hair neatly plaited into braids and tied with ribbons, their high-buttoned boots skipping along the dusty Enmore road. May found those first days of school long and tiring, listening to the drone of the bees outside and the drone of the older students repeating lessons inside. It was a relief when lunch hour came and she and Maggie could share their lunches, each of them offering her favourite sandwiches or sweets to the other, while sitting on the grass in the cool shadow of the schoolhouse. They also shared their childhood secrets, promising not to tell another soul what was closest to their hearts. They were kindred spirits, these two, and in their child's hearts they knew it would be so for all their lives.

The girls studied for ten years at Enmore School. May was always very shy and would rather have been at home with Mama and Papa and Old Grandfather and Old Grandmother. When thunderstorms came she sometimes became so nervous that she had to go to the house closest to the school to wait them out in the safety of a neighbour's kitchen. Maggie was always allowed to go with her for company. Having a best friend made everything easier. As they grew older they began to enjoy school life, learning to read and memorize poetry, learning about the great wide world outside of Enmore and Prince Edward Island. Recess and lunch hour became fun, playing games or building houses in the trees around the school.

When May and Maggie finished grade ten, their lives went in different directions. May went off to Prince of Wales College to study to become a teacher. She was still very shy and found it lonesome so far from her Enmore home and her family. She missed Maggie, who was soon to be married to Reuben Enman. Long letters were exchanged, telling of their lives as they were now and always sharing the secrets of their hearts.

After graduating, May was asked to teach in her home school, Enmore. She was afraid the students, most of whom had so recently been her schoolmates, would resent having her as their teacher. She was happily surprised at how well they accepted her. Her first year as a teacher was very successful. She spent many happy hours that spring and summer going for long walks down the Enmore road with Maggie, sharing their dreams for the future.

For the next six years, May taught in Chelton, Milburn, St. Eleanors and then Springhill. Her school in Springhill was right beside her dear friend's home. Maggie and Reuben had two children now, a boy and a girl. The friendship didn't need to be revived. They had kept it alive with letters through all the years of rarely seeing one another. When they sat down in Maggie's kitchen, they were just like those two little girls walking hand-in-hand to school. Once again they shared what was closest to their hearts, holding nothing back. May told Maggie of her love for her childhood sweetheart which was beginning to grow into more than just a dream. Maggie told May of the sweet joy of motherhood.

Then disaster struck. These were the years when tuberculosis was rampant in the world. New cases were being discovered every day. When Maggie was diagnosed, both she and May could hardly accept what this could mean. Maggie was young, had always been healthy. May had always been the frail one. But they had to accept it, as Maggie kept getting sicker and sicker. She was told that she could no longer live in the same house as her husband and her children. They might catch it from her. So Reub built her a little house beside their home. Her children were only allowed to talk with her through the window, they were not to go inside her house. It was too dangerous. Their mother's sickness was extremely contagious.

Many people began to implore May not to visit Maggie. It was too much of a risk they said, for someone who was so small and thin and wasn't strong enough to fight off illness. May could not accept this. She knew she was much stronger than she appeared. She also knew that Maggie needed her, and she needed Maggie. Most people were afraid to visit as Maggie grew weaker and weaker, the tuberculosis eating away at her. It became harder for her to speak and even to breathe. May continued to visit her every day after school until she was taken to hospital. When Maggie would struggle to speak, May would sit quietly beside her and tell her stories of their childhood and their old school chums and all the fun they had at Enmore School. Sometimes May could still make her laugh, remembering the good times they had together as children. They shared the secrets of their hearts until the last, as they had always done, as they had known they always would. When death came, Maggie accepted it calmly and with great courage.

May had many dear friends in her lifetime, but she cherished her first friendship her whole life. Even in her last years, speaking of Maggie brought a smile to her eyes, remembering.

Bumps in the Night

Once when May and Annie were teenagers, Maude Enman came to visit with Annie and spend the night. This always meant trouble for May as Maude and Annie were prone to tease when they got together, and who better to tease than the younger sister.

On the same day that Maude arrived, Herb Nesbitt dropped in, planning to spend the night at Toff and Liza's. Any other time, Annie would have been allowed to use the spare bedroom downstairs to entertain her guest. Of course an adult must be considered first, so instead of the spare room the girls would be sleeping in their own bedroom, three girls in the one bed.

That evening May, Annie and Maude walked to a Young People's meeting in Victoria West Church. Annie and Maude accepted an offer for a ride home in Myrick MacKenzie's wagon just after the meeting, assuming that May would walk home with the Frost girls or some of the Enmore crowd who had been at the church.

Of course, Annie and Maude arrived home first. They had told May that they would wait up for her, feeling quite sure that she would forget that Herb would be sleeping in the downstairs bedroom. They intended to be awake to sneak downstairs and watch what happened when May went to the guest room expecting to find them there. They went to bed to chat and giggle and wait for the fun.

When May came into the house, it was all in darkness as everyone, including her parents, had gone to bed. Expecting to surprise Annie and Maude in the middle of sharing secrets, she forgot all about Herb, just as they had imagined she would. She thought they were pretending to be asleep and ran into the downstairs bedroom, jumping on the bottom of the bed, calling out: "You're trying to fool me, you're trying to fool me!"

Herb woke from a sound sleep, shouting: "What, what, who is it?"

Horrified, May tried to explain, then decided the best way out of this was just to escape. She tore up the stairs to the bedroom she shared with Annie, dying of embarrassment and imagining how mercilessly they would tease her this time. She found them sleeping peacefully, with no idea of how well their plan had worked.

"Well," thought May, "I'll never tell them!"

The next morning at the breakfast table, totally unaware of the proceedings of the night before, Toff asked Herb, "So, how did you sleep last night, Herb?" The answer was: "I would have slept all right if the women would have left me alone. They jumped all over me." Oh the smirks on the faces of two of those "women." And how they enjoyed watching May's face turn red with embarrassment.

Whether or not Herb and Toff ever got an explanation remains a mystery.

A CHRISTMAS FEAST

Christmas Eve dawned cold and clear. I was whistling and humming happily as I finished the barn chores. Walking toward the house I could almost smell the plum pudding, bubbling in its can on the back of the stove. There would be bread and buns coming out of the oven, and Mama would be getting the stuffing ready for the Christmas goose. She'd have running spruce, wrapped with bright red cranberries she'd picked in the bog, draped over the doors and windows. The scent of it would be mixing with the smells of cooking and baking. I knew I'd have to stand still at the door for a minute before I stepped inside, just to drink it all in.

The house always had that waiting feeling on the day of Christmas Eve. There would be a great meal at noon today, but not nearly like the one we'd be having tomorrow. Somehow looking forward to it always made it that much better.

May and Annie got home yesterday for Christmas holidays from their teaching jobs. Lots of excitement meeting them at the train in Northam, their arms full of presents and them all smiles. There wasn't much money in the country this fall, so I hadn't made much picking potatoes for the neighbours, but I'd been able to get a new axe-handle for Papa and I'd carved a sparrow for Mama. I think she'll like it. She's always so delighted when I make her something. I found scarves for the girls at Reub Enman's store that only cost ten cents each. They'll be happy with the bright colours. Christmas morning isn't as exciting as when I was small, but it's fun getting presents for the family. The five of us around the tree, laughing and teasing as we open our gifts, is the best part of Christmas for me.

Perhaps since the chores are all done until evening I'll be able to spend the afternoon visiting around. The girls will be busy helping Mama with the baking. Maybe I'll go across the fields to see what the MacLaurin boys are up to. Perhaps I'll walk down to Noye's later. That house is sure to be full of music on Christmas Eve. Papa might come along and bring his fiddle. Oh, probably not! He has a terrible cold. He wouldn't want to be spreading it around, especially not on Christmas Eve.

Papa was already in his rocking chair when I stepped into the kitchen. He'd left the finishing up in the barn to me because he wasn't feeling all that well. I was just about to suggest that I was going to spend the day visiting. Before I got a word out, Papa said: "I hate to ask you to do this Sid, it being Christmas Eve, but I need that load of lumber delivered to the sawmill in Portage. They said they could saw it this afternoon if I'd get it there this morning. I've got such a head full of cold that I just can't face that bitter wind along the back shore road. This must be the coldest Christmas Eve we've had in years."

"No Christmas cheer for me," I thought glumly. But I knew Papa must be really sick or he would be going himself. Instead of spending the day setting rabbit traps with the MacLaurins or singing with the Noye boys, I would be taking a long windy trip with the bobsleigh along the back shore road to Portage.

Papa gave me some good advice before I went to hitch up the horses. He told me to be sure to stop on the way back and get warmed up, warning me that my fingers might freeze on the reins if I tried to make it both ways without stopping. The horses would be needing a rest too because they'd be hauling a heavy load and the snow would be deep in places. Aunt Emma's in Portage would be a good place to stop. He knew she'd be right glad to see me and I could warm up good there before I started back.

What a cold, hard ride it was. The snow from the horse's hooves was thrown back in my face and it wasn't long till I was nearly frozen. At least the horses weren't cold. Their backs steamed with sweat from the effort of hauling. I'd been taught from a very young age to take good care of the horses, so I watched them closely. Their hard breathing made great puffs of smoke in the wintry air, but the way they tossed their manes made me think they were enjoying the winter day. Sometimes the shore road was almost drifted over and the horses would nearly flounder. They were wading almost up to their bellies in places, straining with their strong shoulder muscles to keep the load moving. It seemed like we would never make it to Portage, the hours dragging by like days. My fingers were freezing inside my doubled wool mitts, and I felt like I'd never be warm again.

Finally, with the logs delivered, I pulled the horses up in front of Aunt Emma and Uncle John Durant's. Their little house was tucked into the woods by the side of the road. The minute I called out "Whoa" to the horses the door opened, spilling dogs and cousins onto the doorstep. Aunt Emma and Uncle John were right behind. What a warm welcome!

"Sid, whatever are you doing out on this cold day, lad? Come in, come in, and warm yourself by the fire. The boys'll see to the horses," Uncle John declared. Aunt Emma bustled me inside, close to the stove. "Take that coat off and let me hang it over a chair by the stove till the snow melts off it. Ach, your mitts are frozen stiff and your hands must be, too! Get your bones warmed up by that good fire and when you're thawed out you'll have a bite to eat with us," Aunt Emma insisted.

I looked around the small kitchen, from the hand-made table and chairs to the old iron cookstove, back to where Uncle John sat rocking and smoking his pipe. The small room was filled up with my Durant cousins, three boys and eight girls. They all found spots around the kitchen, some two-to-a-chair, some curled up on the floor, while I sat with my feet on the oven door.

I knew that the two oldest boys, Charlie and Jimmy, were away in the lumber woods in Maine for the winter. They'd be dearly missed at Christmas time, but the lumber camps didn't take much time off to celebrate. They wouldn't have enough time to make the long trip to the Island, for sure.

Aunt Emma and Uncle John were anxious to hear all the news from Enmore. They wanted to know how Mama and Papa were doing, and how the girls were getting along at their teaching. When I told them why Papa couldn't come himself, Emma was sorry to hear her younger brother wasn't well. "We'll have to try to get to Enmore in the spring of the year," she said in that soft old-country lilt that I loved to hear. "We'll have a good long visit with them then."

Emma had been a teenager when Toff was born and married by the time he was starting school, but she had always had a soft spot in her heart for her baby brother. She had become good friends with Liza too, even with the difference in years. They had much in common, those two, for they had both married for love in a time when that wasn't always the case. Emma was happy that her little brother had found someone who loved him as deeply and dearly as she loved her John.

Aunt Emma bustled about, laying the table for the noon meal. I wondered what it was we would eat. It had been a long time since breakfast and my stomach was beginning to grumble. There wasn't much evidence of anything cooking, just a pot of potatoes on the back of the stove. I knew they didn't have much, John and Emma, and a big family to feed. Uncle John and the boys earned their living fishing from spring until fall. In winter they trapped fox and rabbit and whatever else they could snare. They didn't get a lot for the pelts, but every bit of cash helped. They made a bit of money by cutting cedar for fence posts, as well. With a houseful of youngsters to feed they wouldn't have much left over for buying anything from the store.

Emma set the table and soon she called out a cheery "Sit in, sit in!" The whole family found a place at the long table. Onto the table came a large bowl of boiled potatoes and a shaker of salt. The bowl was passed from plate to plate with the salt dish following after it. We ate and talked and laughed together until every bit was gone. Emma poured cups of strong tea and my stomach, if not filled, was not quite so empty. Not only were my fingers and toes warmed up but my spirits, which had been so low on that long cold Christmas Eve ride, were in much better shape. Uncle John reached for his fiddle to give me a Christmas tune to cheer my way home. Nothing would do but I had to join my cousins in a reel around the kitchen. We danced until we were falling into our chairs laughing, our heads spinning.

This Christmas Eve day that had started out so badly had turned into one I would remember my whole life. I left that little house with a fiddle tune in my head and a smile on my face that lasted all the way home. Uncle John and Aunt Emma had little by way of worldly goods, but what they had they offered gladly and without apology. Potatoes and salt. A Christmas feast shared with family!

FROST CHRISTMAS

(A memory from Eva)

A sky full of stars shone down on the Frost home in Enmore on that special night. Four sisters and one brother were snuggled into their beds, wondering in whispers what Santa might bring. This Christmas, perhaps 1916, was celebrated in the old house. In a few years there would be a new house on the Frost farm. There would also be a new baby brother, to complete the Frost family. On this wondrous night in the Frost household, there was the quiet of the stars and the excitement of anticipation. What would Santa Claus bring?

The five children went early to bed this Christmas Eve, but not early to sleep. There was too much to think about, too much to imagine. Just before bed they had hung their hand-knit woolen stockings on a clothesline stretched across a corner of the kitchen, near the stove. Long before daylight they woke, ran downstairs, grabbed their socks from the line and scampered back to their beds, which had already lost their warmth. The wood fire would have been out for a few hours by now, so the house would be very cold.

While Mom and Papa tried to get a bit more sleep the stockings would be dug into, each child announcing the treasures found inside—an orange, an apple, peanuts in the shell, hard candy. There was a book for each of the older girls, Marjorie and Jessie, and a jack-knife for Charlie. The two littlest girls, Eva and Anna, found homemade cloth dolls in their stockings. A few years later Marjorie would help Mom make dolls for them with dresses and yarn for hair. One year they were delighted to get "store-bought" dolls, dressed as boys. They gave them boy's names—Frank and Ralph. It wasn't long until they dressed the dolls as girls and changed their names to Susie and Dora.

Aunt Eva Abbott and her family, who lived in the States, sometimes sent books, crayons, ribbons and barretts for the girls and perhaps a book for Charlie. This Christmas box was the cause of great excitement, as gifts were few in farm homes where money was always scarce.

When the new house was built in 1920 there was a Christmas tree for the first time. The new baby brother, Lloyd, had arrived in April. Charlie, who was eleven years old that year, went to the brook and found a fir tree along the bank. The MacLaurin boys went with him and they proudly brought their trees home for decorating. Mom and the girls made decorations from crepe paper and they strung cranberries to drape on the tree. There were candle holders with real candles that clipped onto the branches. The candles were a fire hazard so Papa was relieved when the tree came down.

The special Christmas dinner would be roast pork with gravy, mashed potatoes, vegetables, cranberry sauce, crabapple pickles. For dessert there would be plum pudding, which had been steamed in a bag, covered in vanilla sauce.

Christmas afternoon Papa would hitch a horse to the wood sleigh and put straw in the box. Mom would put in a blanket and the buffalo robe and the youngsters would crawl under these covers and make a nest. Mom and Papa would sit on the seat up front. If the bay was frozen they would go across the ice to North Enmore to visit the Murray's. Mary and John Murray were old enough to be grandparents but had never had children of their own. Jessie was the quiet one of the Frost family and seemed to be their favourite. The other children teased Anna on the way home because Mr. Murray always called her Hannah. When they got home, after the sleigh ride across the ice with the stars twinkling above, most of the children would be asleep and have to be carried to their beds.

The Frost Christmas was a quiet one, but the day was a big event for the children, which they looked forward to for weeks. They were never disappointed in the magic it brought.

WE SURE HAD FUN

On a moonlit night in summer or early fall, laughter would echo in the air. The quick step of feet could be heard, heading down the road to the North Enmore bridge. Almost every house would have one or two to add to the group. There were lots of young people in rural communities back then. When they reached the bridge, someone would be asked to "tune." Tuning was a very particular talent. It had to be a boy with a strong voice and a head full of fiddle music who could keep a rhythm going for as long as the dancers had breath to dance. He would make the music of the fiddle, "diddle-diddle-dum-tara-diddle-diddle-dum" to the beat of all the tunes he knew, one after another. One boy would tune for as long as his breath held out and then another would give him a "spell." All the other boys and girls would dance the night away on the bridge, beneath the moon and the stars.

There was lots of music in Enmore—no shortage of fiddlers along the Enmore Road. Some homes had a piano or an organ, but almost every house had a fiddle. Toff Enman would sit on his veranda on a summer's eve and play his fiddle while the courting couples would be driving by. It wouldn't be long till the yard would be filled with wagons and the field in front of the house would become a dance floor. The dancing would go on as long as Toff's arm held out or until the moon set, whichever came first. Many a romance got its start to the music of Lord MacDonald's reel on the Enmore Road.

Dances were sometimes organized in the Enmore

Hall. There would be a fiddler, of course, and dancers of all ages would form a square set and dance the night away. Most everyone from the road would be there and some from North Enmore and Victoria West, too. Little children would come along with their parents. There were no baby-sitters because the grandparents wanted to dance. As the night wore on the youngest ones would be tucked up in a blanket on the benches or on a corner of the floor, sound asleep, while the music never stopped. There were times when more than one Enmore farmer had to change his clothes and go right to the barn for the morning milking when the dance was over.

When the square dance had everyone out of breath, the fiddler would slow down to a waltz rhythm. The bravest young couples would pair off and join the older generation on the dance floor. Some of those older couples would have been practising their steps together for forty or fifty years. The talk in the hall would quiet to a hush and the whole gathering would seem to hold their breath as the dancers swept around the floor like trees swaying in the wind.

Dancing was just one way for boys and girls to enjoy one another's company. Those young men who were old enough to borrow the family driving wagon came up with another form of entertainment. Every lad was sure his horse could outrun any other horse in Enmore and there was a good straight stretch of road from Enman's to Frost's. The only problem was the older generation watching from behind their kitchen curtains. There was a danger that driving privileges could be lost if the wrong person had a chat with father after church on Sunday. Even worse, a courtship might have to come to an abrupt end if the young lady's parents were to hear of this reckless behaviour. But oh, the excitement of racing your wagon as fast as your horse could go, down the Enmore Road to the North Enmore Bridge!

On a Sunday afternoon in summer a group of friends might walk down to the shore which bordered the farm fields on the south side of the Enmore Road. There were always dories pulled up out of the water or anchored at the water's edge. Most Enmore people built their own boats, both dories and sailboats. Launching one of those boats to go for a row or a sail on a sunny summer day was a great way for couples to pair off. No one was ever left behind, coupled or not. Younger sisters and brothers would always tag along. There would be quite a range of ages, from eight or ten to maybe sixteen or seventeen. There might be a chance for a flirting couple to hold hands, or even sneak a quick kiss at the back of the dory when everyone else was watching the waves or peering into the water to look for quahaugs. Those July days at

Ed Enman's Shore or Frost Creek were remembered happily in later years when the Enmore folk came together from wherever their lives had taken them.

A play or concert was a winter entertainment enjoyed by the people in Enmore. Rehearsals were held in homes, every actor or actress taking their turn at hosting. There would always be a lunch to end the evening and sometimes a kitchen square dance. The plays were usually funny and the tricks the actors played on one another were even funnier. Costumes disappeared at the last minute. Prompted lines had nonsense added to them, which the younger actors and actresses repeated faithfully. Only when everyone broke into unexpected laughter did they realize they had been tricked. Of course it wasn't long before the young ones learned tricks of their own. Everyone was kept on their toes, never knowing what would happen next. Perhaps that was why it was so easy to recruit actors for the plays … or it could have been because the young men would always very gallantly offer to walk the girls home at the end of the evening. Another chance for romance on the Enmore Road.

On spring evenings after chores were done the Enmore youngsters would often have a ball game. The bat would probably be made from a small board whittled down at the bottom to make a handgrip. Sometimes they had a rubber ball, but mostly they just made their own with yarn. They made their own rules too, which were changed to fit the number of players. The games would be played in a field after the hay was cut or sometimes in a farmyard. Once in a while a father would come along and join in. Alf Frost once impressed them all by hitting the ball over the top of the barn. If there were too many extras for the teams, the youngest ones would play tag. When it got too dark to see the ball, everybody would join in the game of tag, until they were all tired out and ready to be home for bed.

One spring evening after the ballgame, the game of tag became a game of "grab-the-hat." It was a free-for-all in which everyone was snatching everyone else's hat and playing "keep-away" with it. Not many of the Enmore young folk knew that one of the ball players, Eva Frost, had been nicknamed "Dimples" by her teacher, Eva Sabine. The teacher came walking along the road just as this game was ending and everyone was trying to find their hat so they could go home. Seeing Eva Frost searching for her hat, her teacher stopped to help, suspecting one of the boys was hiding it. Eva Sabine walked over to Les Noye and asked, "Do you have Dimple's?" Les was quite surprised by this question but after a few seconds he admitted, "Well, I guess I've got one." The teacher got a great laugh out of that, but poor Les was quite embarrassed when he realized that she had really been asking him if he had taken Dimple's hat.

When there are lots of young folk close enough to get together easily it's not difficult to have fun any time of the year. The young people of Enmore walked wherever they wanted to go, no matter if it was a few miles. The walk to and from an event was often as much fun as the event itself.

THE WORLD BEYOND ENMORE

In the early nineteen-hundreds life in Enmore was sometimes a quiet existence. There were ball games, dances, boat rides, and walks to the shore when the day's work was done, but the daily routine was one of long hours and hard work. However, with school and lots of chores to do on the farm, Enmore's young folk certainly had no time to be bored.

Most Enmore people of this time knew very little of the wider world. For some, there was no desire to know more than what they read in the newspapers. But for others there was a curiosity about what else was out there.

Growing up in Enmore left young people with few options for making a living. For girls there was teaching or nursing if you had money to get the training, or marrying a man who would provide for you. For the young men in the family the options were even more limited. You could work on your father's farm with the hope that he would let you take over when he was no longer able to do the work himself. That option worked best for the youngest son because the father would have to provide for his family until the girls had all married and the older boys had all found other employment. That could take a while.

In the family of Alfred and Christy Frost there were four girls and two boys. Providing some kind of training for all of them was out of the question, given the limited resources of a small farm. So as each of the older Frost children came of an age to make a living, they chose to leave Prince Edward Island to look for employment in the eastern United States. Many of their friends had already gone to New York, Maine or Massachusetts, so they had contacts who might possibly be able to help them find work. The older girls settled in Augusta, Maine, at least for awhile. Charlie went on to New York, where he soon found himself working on the construction of the New York City subway.

Every summer the girls and Charlie would return to the farm for a short vacation. Lloyd was too young to be a part of this out-migration and no doubt his father hoped he would stay home and take over the farm.

In 1936, Lloyd was seventeen years old and, like most of the Enmore folk, had never been off Prince Edward Island. That summer Anna and Eva came home in Eva's Model A Ford. Eva did most of the driving as Anna was not good at shifting gears and always started with rabbit-hops. Anna loved driving, so she was very happy when automatic transmissions were finally invented years later.

Eva was planning to stay on Prince Edward Island until November that year. Anna needed to go back to work and she wanted company and help in driving back to Augusta. Lloyd was seven years younger than Anna, but somehow she persuaded Alf and Christy to let Lloyd go back with her to help her drive … even though he had no licence. He had learned to drive, having been allowed to drive around Enmore in Eva's car all summer. Not having a licence was not considered an obstacle by the three young people, so Alf and Christy were persuaded to let Lloyd go. No doubt they were worried about Anna driving that long way back by herself.

Bright and early one fine morning, Lloyd and Anna set out for Augusta. There were no paved roads in 1936, except for the main streets in towns and cities.

The highway went through the heart of every town and city, all the way to Augusta. They left Enmore early in the morning, driving through Summerside to Borden where they caught the ferry. They drove through Moncton, Sussex, down to St. Andrews-By-the-Sea, because that's where the road went. It was all gravelled road. They stopped in Rothesay the first night. Next morning they set off again with high spirits. They got lost in St. John, but that didn't dampen their enthusiasm. Soon they were on their way to St. Stephen and Calais. At this point, fear began to settle in the pit of Lloyd's stomach. He told himself not to worry. He was armed with letters of recommendation from the bank manager, the minister, and the Justice of the Peace (who just happened to be the Frost's neighbour, Toff Enman). Still, Lloyd wondered what would happen at the border. Would they let him cross into the United States? He didn't have long to wait for his answer. He and Anna both breathed a sigh of relief when they got through Calais without any questioning.

While Lloyd was driving, Anna insisted he stay at a speed of forty miles per hour. The roads were gravel and all washboards, so he had to reluctantly agree that that wasn't such a bad idea. 'The Airline' hadn't been improved at this point in time. Anna decided that rather than take the shore route, which was winding and slow, they would head north to Topsfield, west to Lincoln, then south to Bangor and Augusta. They arrived in Bangor about sunset and had pavement all the way from there to Augusta. "Some nice!" said Lloyd.

Jessie and Frank were waiting to show Lloyd the town as soon as they arrived. It was quite an experience to see all the traffic and the bright lights! Lloyd was especially amazed at the flashing rows of lights on the theatre marquees. Augusta sure was bigger and brighter than Summerside.

Lloyd spent about two weeks in Augusta, visiting at Jessie's and Marjorie's and occasionally at Mr. Hitchborn's where Anna worked. During this time he was taken to the top of the State House and to lots of movies. He even had a ride in a small airplane. He went to Old Orchard Beach, where he rode the roller coaster, went through Noah's Ark, and all the other amusements. These were all exciting new experiences for a young man from a small community on the south shore of Prince Edward Island. All of this was paid for by his four sisters. Lloyd felt that not many people in the world were as lucky as he was.

When the time came to return home, he was put on the train for Prince Edward Island with volumes of instructions from his sisters. The train ride was one more new experience and a wonderful ending to a holiday Lloyd remembered for the rest of his life.

GETTING CLEANED UP

Keeping a large family clean, with only a hand pump for water and a warming tank on the side of the wood stove to heat it, could be a challenge. There were no bathrooms in most of the farm houses of the early nineteen-hundreds. Most homes had a portable tub for doing laundry in the daytime and having a bath on Saturday night.

The wood stove was fired up winter and summer, spring and fall. In winter it was the only source of heat for the house, for cooking meals, and for hot water for washing dishes, clothing and bodies. There was a tank on the side of the stove which was kept constantly full of water from the pump, so that hot water was available whenever it was needed. It was usually the job of the younger children to make sure that tank was always full. In summer, though no longer required to heat the house, the fire was still necessary for cooking and washing clothing and keeping clean. It can only be imagined what it must have been like on a steaming hot July day with the wood stove going full blast. No matter the heat, floors must be scrubbed (on hands and knees), dishes and clothing washed. All of these necessary chores required hot water.

The washtub with its scrub board would be taken outside as soon as the weather was warm enough. Getting away from the heat of the kitchen to wash the clothes would be a blessed relief. Hanging clothes on the line to dry was a welcome chance to enjoy the summer sunshine and hopefully a pleasant breeze. Hanging clothes out in winter was another story. The overalls, pinafores, long underwear and wool socks would be carried in, frozen stiff as boards, to be hung behind the stove or around the kitchen to thaw. Hanging them outside was necessary to get as much water out of them as possible so that they would dry faster inside, without having water drip all over the floor.

Having a bath was for Saturday night only, so as to be clean for church on Sunday. There was pride on the mother's face who could walk her children into church on Sunday morning with spanking clean faces, all dressed up in their best Sunday clothing.

One Enmore mother, in particular, took great pride in keeping her house and her large family clean. Her watchword to her children was, "We may not have much money, but we can afford soap." They lived in a rambling old farmhouse which had been built in more prosperous days. There were two sets of stairs in their house—the kitchen stairs and the parlour stairs. The parlour stairs were rarely used. The parlour was reserved for company, especially for visiting with the minister or people "home from away." The children were Certainly Not Allowed to go up one stairs and down the other. Of course, this made it a forbidden pleasure to be enjoyed only when Mama wasn't watching.

The youngest children spent their summer days playing outside—running through mud puddles, in and out of the barn and hen house, through the fields and along the brook. They caught and examined frogs and toads and other interesting creatures. They built playhouses in the woods and came home covered with tree sap. They ran down to the shore to dig clams, filling their hair and pockets with sand. There were so many good opportunities to get really dirty on a farm on the Enmore Road!

When bedtime came, their mother would line them up at the kitchen sink, youngest to oldest. She would take a dipper full of water out of the warming tank on the side of the wood stove, pour it into the face pan in the sink, get a clean facecloth just dry off the clothesline, and proceed to help her children wash themselves before bed. "Up as far as possible and down as far as possible" was how she explained it to them, meaning that they didn't really need to wash the parts hidden by their clothes. That was for Saturday night bath time. So their faces, necks, and ears, both inside and out, were scoured first. Then the work began on the grubby little hands and feet that had travelled so far and experienced so much throughout the day. As each young body passed inspection after the scrubbing was finished, they were sent up the kitchen stairs to bed.

Toff Enman was visiting this neighbour one summer evening as this procedure was taking place. He was sitting in the kitchen rocking chair, discussing politics with the man of the house. Having only three children of his own, he couldn't help but keep one eye on the washing ritual of this large family. He soon realized that the line of children didn't seem to be getting much shorter. The mother's mind must have been distracted with the political talk that evening, because her boys were going up the kitchen stairs and coming down the parlour stairs and around to the kitchen sink to get in line for the second time. When she had washed the third or fourth boy twice, they could keep their laughter in no longer. "Oh, pshaw," she said, "Get off to bed with you! Do you think I got nothin' better to do than wash your ears all night!" The last one got a smack on the bottom, and off they went, giggling at the trick they'd played on their mother.

In a week or two, when her mind was occupied by the million things she had to do before she got to bed herself, they'd play that same trick on her all over again. On an Enmore farm with lots of children cleanliness may have been next to godliness, but it was also almost next to impossible!

BILL AND CHARLIE

Charlie Frost and his friend, Bill Baglole, were experts in the field of mischief. Whatever the circumstance or event, these two could find a way to pull a trick on someone. When the boys were about twelve years old, an evangelical group set up a big tent in a field in Mount Pleasant. They advertised evenings of preaching by famous evangelists from somewhere far from PEI. One and all were invited to come along to Hear the Word and Be Saved. Announcements were made in the churches, posted in the store at the Corner, on the door of the sawmill, and everywhere else people of the surrounding communities might gather. There was lots of talk about who these people were, but since the churches were promoting it, most people thought it must be alright to go and see.

By seven o'clock that evening the tent couldn't possibly have held one more person. People of all ages were there, but the crowd was mostly adults. Parents probably felt that the preaching might be too intense for young children. Most of the people who were seated on benches inside the tent had come there with sincere intentions. Some were, no doubt, troubled about the state of their souls. Some were there for the fire-and-brimstone preaching they couldn't wait to hear, perhaps hoping to be stirred up to become better versions of themselves. A few may have been there to see which of their neighbours would "go to the front" to publicly declare their desire to be saved. Possibly there were a few who attended in the hope that this tent meeting might turn into a real show, in which people would be possessed by the Spirit to the point where they would be in a state of ecstasy, jumping and screaming and rolling on the ground. That kind of entertainment would be worth getting dressed up for!

Those most sincerely interested in the message were seated closest to the front. They were the ones who had arrived first and those front seats had filled up quickly. The women were wearing their best dresses and flowered hats and the men wore the suits and ties that were normally reserved for Sunday morning or funerals. At the very back of the tent, with their heads leaning against the canvas, sat a group of older men whose reasons for attending were varied. Some were there reluctantly, because their wives had insisted they come along and 'get some religion into ya, for heaven's sake!' Others may have been among those hoping for some entertainment. Whatever their reasons, they relaxed against the canvas and swapped stories, waiting for the "show" (as they hoped it would be) to begin.

They hadn't long to wait. The first speaker was introduced and it was no time before the hoped-for fire and brimstone was riveting the imaginations of the crowd. The whole gathering was swept up in the conviction and emotion thundering at them from the professional evangelists on stage.

The folks were so caught up in the performance that no one noticed two boys outside the back of the tent. Two boys with small sticks in their hands. As the preaching reached a fever pitch, the boys looked at one another and whispered, "Now!" The two of them began to run along the back of the tent, one behind the other, where those heads were leaning into the canvas. As they ran they smacked as hard as they could without slowing down. "Whap-Whap-Whap" went those sticks on the lumps made by the balding heads. In seconds the occupants of that back row erupted like hornets from a nest, roaring and shouting! Out of the tent they spilled, stumbling and tripping in a mad dash to catch those young whipper-snappers and give them a good boot! They could see the scallywags making a dead run for the Tommy Cod Road. They were close enough to catch, but aging men in Sunday shoes are no match for ten-year-old boys with their escape route all figured out. The boys were probably half way to Enmore before those old men ever hit their stride.

I'm not sure how the rest of the preaching went that night, but fifty years later Bill and Charlie still laughed till the tears ran down their faces when they told this story.

"They were mad as hornets, all right!"

"Did ya see them rubbing their heads?"

"No, I was running too fast."

"One of them could run pretty fast. Nearly caught me!"

"Glad they didn't get close enough to recognize us."

"Whose idea was that anyway?"

Charlie and Bill looked at each other and at the same time they both said: "Yours."

When the opportunity offered, the two tricksters were not above playing a trick on one another. When they were of an age to begin courting, they often 'double dated.' This would mean that one of the two would borrow his father's buggy and they would take their girls out driving. After a while, Bill was beginning to get quite serious about his girl and decided that he would like to spend an evening alone with her. So he invited her to go out one evening, without mentioning his plan to Charlie. Of course, driving down the Enmore Road, Charlie saw his friend's buggy tied to the fence in her father's yard. Charlie just drove on by, picked up his date, and spent a lovely evening rambling down around the shore. Later, he sat on the verandah with his girl, watching the moon come up … and go down. On his way home in the wee hours of the morning, he noticed Bill's buggy still tied to the fence at the MacArthur farm. So he tied his horse and wagon at the end of the lane, walked up into the yard and unhitched Bill's horse. He led the horse down the lane and tied it to the back of his own wagon, leaving Bill's wagon beside the fence where he found it. Then he drove to Bill's home and led the horse into the field beside the barn, where he was happy to get out of his harness and roll in the dew-wet grass. Of course, when Bill decided it was time to go home, he was very surprised to find that he had a buggy but no horse to pull it. The sun was starting to peek over the horizon when a footsore Bill finally arrived home to find his horse contentedly grazing in the pasture field beside the barn. On that long walk, Bill had had plenty of time to plot his revenge!

For the next few weeks Charlie was very nervous, waiting for the inevitable. Finally, he said to Bill, "Would you just do what you're going to do and get it over with!"

"Why would I need to do anything? You have no idea how much I've enjoyed watching you squirm, waiting for me to pull something on you. Maybe I'll never get revenge, but maybe I will and you'll never know when it might be coming or what it's going to be, will you? I might just keep you second-guessing for a long time!"

A College Year in Charlottetown

What a year this would be! May was going to Charlottetown ... and not just for a day. She was going to be a student at Prince of Wales. Annie had gone last year to take teacher training and would be starting her teaching career this fall. She had told May about the fun of boarding with other girls, the hard work of studying for exams, the strangeness of living in a town with no fields around, houses so close together. It would all be new to May and it was very exciting ... and a little scary.

Young women on Prince Edward Island in the early 1900's had few options open to them for their future. In farming communities like Enmore, a son usually took over the farm and eventually married. This meant that any daughters in the household were in the difficult position of finding a home of their own, or of being an unpaid maid in the home they grew up in. It was possible for this to work out very well, if a young woman had no desire for a family of her own and if she got along well with the sister-in-law who had become the lady of the house. She might be quite content to remain at home to look after her parents as they aged and to help with the babies of her brother's family. Many young women, however, wanted a home of their own, but jobs for females were few and far between. Unless they were willing to move to a city, marriage seemed to be their only option. Some young women of this time married for the wrong reasons, feeling that there was nothing else they could do.

Toff Enman had spent several winters working in

the lumber woods of New Brunswick and Maine in order to earn the money to send his two daughters to Prince of Wales College to become teachers. He wanted his girls to have choices, to be independent. He had an only son to inherit his farm. Thus it was possible for him to invest his hard-earned money from winters in the woods into education for his daughters. Toff was happy to be able to do this for his girls. He knew this would not have been an option if he and Liza had had a larger family. As it was, he was grateful to Liza for being willing to do without much that may have made her life easier, so that the girls could have an education. Toff was proud of his girls and he knew they would work hard to succeed in their studies.

The summer that Eva Frost was fifteen years old, her sister Marjorie was home from "the States" on vacation. She suggested to her parents that it might be wise for Eva to get some training before she joined her sisters in Augusta, Maine, to look for work. Marjorie thought that Eva might go to business school in Charlottetown, which would prepare her for work in an office. Knowing that her parents couldn't afford to give their four daughters a college education, and suspecting that they wouldn't wish to seem to be favouring one of the girls over the others, Marjorie offered to pay Eva's tuition. She even offered to pay for the necessary room and board.

Union Commercial College was a good business school and close enough to Prince of Wales that May and Eva could board together. May's sister, Annie, had boarded at the Jenkins house the year before when she attended Prince of Wales for her teacher training course. May had visited the College when Annie was a student there and had also visited Annie's boarding house. She had gone on the train with her father when Annie went to Charlottetown for the first time. Having had this opportunity to experience life beyond her country home, May was excited about beginning her year at Prince of Wales. She was happy that Eva would be sharing a room in the boarding house with her, though. It would be good to be able to talk together about their families and friends in Enmore.

Eva had never been on a train, and had only seen a train once or twice, so she was happy to have May to answer her questions about the train ride and also about what Annie had told May of life in the city of Charlottetown. Everything about this experience was new to Eva and she found it very exciting … and a little scary.

May and Eva's room was on the second floor of the Jenkins house. It was a big room with two windows that looked out on Grafton Street, with Prince of Wales College just across the street. There were two beds, one for Eva and May and the other for their roommates, Verna Darrach and Annie MacGowan. On the third floor, there were two more bedrooms, one rented by two working men and the other by Ralph Linkletter and Gordon Darrach, who were also Prince of Wales students. Gordon was Verna's brother.

Eva had a longer walk in the mornings, since her pals only had to cross the street to get to Prince of Wales. She eventually learned a shortcut and on really cold winter days, there was a Provincial Building that she could duck into to warm her hands on the radiators. The shortcut with its convenient warm-up spot was suggested to Eva by girls she met in her business classes. She was happy to be making new friends at school. It made being away from her family and her familiar life in Enmore a little bit easier. Some of the friendships she made at Union Commercial College lasted a lifetime.

May was also enjoying life at college, although she was desperately lonesome at first. She and Eva were both happy with their roommates, Verna and Annie. Spending time in such close quarters with people you had just met might have presented problems, but the four girls quickly became great chums.

All four girls came from similar circumstances. None of them had any spending money. On long evenings of study when they got very hungry they would combine their pennies and nickels and go to a nearby bake shop where the kind lady would let them have broken and burned cookies. That got them through to the morning when Mrs. Jenkins would have a good breakfast ready for them.

Eva, May and Verna saw their first movie that winter. Verna's sister took the three girls. When the cartoon came on before the movie, they thought that was the whole thing and would have been quite contented to go home when it was finished. They were in a daze when the movie was over and they all agreed that it was absolutely wonderful! They tried to imagine how they could describe it to their parents, but agreed that it would be impossible.

The girls had very little social life, as they were dedicated to doing well at school so that the money spent to send them would not be wasted. They did go for long walks on the weekends, sometimes out into the country so they could see animals in the fields. They were a bit homesick for their country life, even while enjoying the novelty of living in Charlottetown.

There was a Teacher's Convention in Charlottetown that fall. Annie and Eva Sabine, who taught in Enmore, came to attend it. They were driven by an elderly widower, George Nisbet, one of the few people in the Enmore area who had a car. He was happy to take May and Eva out driving along with Annie and Eva Sabine when they had free time. His choice of places to visit on these drives was a bit unusual. They went to Falconwood Insane Asylum for a guided tour one day. May and Eva were afraid at one point that they might not get out, as they got behind the tour group and were almost lost in the building. Another day, George took them to visit the Prince Edward Island Orphanage. These were not exactly Charlottetown hot spots, but the girls did enjoy the drives around the city.

When they went home for Christmas vacation, it was wonderful to see their families. And what a treat to have real homemade bread again! 'Bought' bread had been a nice novelty at first, but they soon tired of it. Their mothers' home-made bread was so delicious in comparison.

One Sunday evening that winter, the girls went to a church function where they heard a black minister speak. Having lived all their lives in Enmore, this was the first black person they had ever seen. They were so fascinated with the colour of his face and his accent that they could barely remember what he spoke about. While walking back to their boarding house, their talk was all about how difficult it would be to describe him to their parents, who would never have met anyone like him. This was an unforgettable experience which was still talked about years later, after they had met people of many different nationalities.

A lot of teasing went on between the boys on the third floor and the girls on the second floor. One day when the girls went for a walk, they came back to find their room in a shambles. The table was tipped over, the bedclothes were on the floor, chairs were on the beds, books were everywhere. The room was a real mess. The girls decided they would tidy everything up and not say a word about it. The next evening when the boys went out, the girls came up with the idea of balancing a box of snow over their door, so that when the boys pushed the door in, the snow would fall down on them. After they got it all set up, they thought they really should have also short-sheeted the bed. Back up they went, with Eva in the lead. With all the laughter and joking about the reaction they were expecting from their prank, they forgot about the box of snow. When Eva pushed the door open, down came the snow on top of her head! Well, after Eva stopped gasping, they scrambled to get it all cleaned up and reset before the boys came back. The girls had just enough time to get back to their room when they heard someone coming up the stairs. They opened their door just a crack so they would hear the commotion when the snow dropped. To their surprise, it was not Gordon and Ralph returning, but a friend of the boys dropping in to visit. He got the benefit of the snow bath! Assuming that Gordon and Ralph had set him up, he was NOT happy about his dunking. When the boys came home there was a lot of loud conversation on the third floor.

The girls laid low the next day, but "fessed up" that evening, and they all had a good laugh over the mix-up, especially Gordon and Ralph who were delighted that they weren't the ones on the receiving end of the snow. The boys weren't told about Eva's snow experience until years later.

Just before Easter break, Eva became sick with flu and a high temperature. One night she almost passed out going to the bathroom. She became confused and couldn't find her way back in the dark. She called out to May, who found her in the hall and got her back to bed. It was only a couple of days till Eva's classes were done for Easter, so she went home on the train. Then May got jaundice just before her final exams and was very sick throughout her whole exam time. She was really too sick to write them, but if she didn't she would forfeit her whole year. With lots of help and constant encouragement from Verna and Gordon, who were studying for the same exams, she wrote those exams and passed them. May knew that if it hadn't been for her two friends, she would have lost her year and her chance to be a teacher.

When May and Eva went home for Easter, there was a big snowstorm and the train got stuck. They were storm-stayed all night on the train at Freetown. A passenger got off and got apples and cookies from a store to share with everyone, so they didn't starve. Their fathers had to come to Summerside the next day to pick them up with horse and sleigh, as that was as far as the train could get.

That year in Charlottetown was a year of fun and of growing up a bit. In the fall, they all began their working lives. Eva went to Maine to work, eventually married and made her life there, returning to Enmore only in the summers. May became the teacher at the Enmore School, where she had been a student only a year before. It was easy for these two to remain good friends all their lives, as May married Eva's brother, Charlie. Their children were cousins and although they grew up in different countries, they too developed friendships that lasted a lifetime.

Sheep Shearing

"Get up now," Pop called from the bottom of the stairs. "We've got a big day ahead of us. Toff is coming over to help with the shearing so we've got to get the sheep into the barn. Get up and have breakfast, quick!" In minutes there was a scramble of young bodies rushing downstairs. They could hardly wait to get their breakfast into them before they were running to the barn. Sheep shearing day was exciting! Perhaps that was because it was a once-a-year task, different from the usual chores and there was lots of running and chasing involved.

The big double barn doors had to be opened before the sheep and lambs could be driven into the farmyard from their pasture. The whole family was needed to stand guard so that the sheep couldn't run down behind the barn. If they got into the woods it would be really hard to herd them back to the barnyard. All the children had sticks or old brooms to shoo the flock in the right direction, right into the barn floor. The barn floor was the large open area in the front of the barn where the hay wagon would be backed in to put the hay in the loft. There were big double doors that opened when that area of the barn was being used. On shearing day Pop had an old wooden door across two sawhorses on the barn floor where the sheep would have to be held down to be sheared.

The lambs had to have their ears notched, which would indicate the farm to which they belonged. This process was quick and relatively painless. The lambs were more bothered by being separated from their mothers while the sheep were being sheared. What a lot of bleating and baaing there would be until ewe and lamb were together again. As each sheep was done, she would be turned loose to find her lamb and oh, the happy wiggling of lamb tails as babies and mothers were reunited. The lambs could only find their mothers by their smell, as the ewes would look so different without their fleece. The little ones would content themselves instantly by suckling, just to make sure. If the mother didn't bunt them away when they tried to suckle they knew they had the right one.

A warm day was always chosen for the shearing as the sheep were losing their heavy winter coats. Every year, it seemed, just after most farmers had their shearing done, there would come a cold rain. Farmers called it the "sheep storm" and were prepared to get the sheep out of the fields and into the barn. Although the sheep were kept inside a shed in winter, they could go into the fields early in spring before shearing because their warm fleece would keep the wind and cold air away from their skin.

When the shearing was done, it fell to the women and girls to pick the twigs and dirt out of the wool. This was a tedious and time-consuming task. When this was done, all the wool was washed outside in a big tub on a warm day and spread on the grass to dry. After the wool was cleaned, it was taken to MacAusland's Woolen Mill in Bloomfield. Some of it was sold to the mill to make blankets, which have since become known world-wide. Some wool was spun into yarn which was used for knitting mittens, socks, and sweaters for the family. Christy would often do the spinning herself on her own small spinning wheel. The knitting would start in the early fall and continue all winter.

A job for the Frost girls and many other Enmore girls, after the shearing was done, was to go to the woods and gather "cruttle." This is a dry, grey-green moss which grows on hardwood trees. There were a few black sheep in the flock and their grey yarn was used as it was, but the white sheep's yarn was dyed. It would be put into a big pot of boiling water with the cruttle and the wool would turn a rusty-orange colour. Lots of rusty-coloured sweaters would be seen at Enmore School when winter came.

Farm life could be monotonous, with all its hard work for the whole family. Shearing brought a bit of excitement because instead of everyone doing their own separate chores, everyone had to work together. There was a lot of running and chasing and everybody had to do their part well to make sure no sheep escaped into the woods. When the sheep were all sheared and the flock were back in their pasture the family would all relax together. There was often a special treat at supper to celebrate a job well done.

Some farm children had pet lambs, but the younger Frost children learned from the older ones that although a little lamb following you around the farm could be fun, a grown sheep following you around and sometimes wanting to come into the house with you was not so much fun any more. They did have one pet lamb whose mother was not feeding it, so it had to be bottle-fed. They named him Bunty because bunting everyone and everything with his hard little head was what he did best. He hung around the yard sometimes, instead of going to the field with the sheep, so he became friends with the family dog, Rags. Bunty and Rags would chase one another around the yard for hours. Then they would lie down together and have a nap in the sun.

The Burning Ship

Five little girls were creeping down the stairwell as quietly as they could. They had been sent to bed about an hour ago, but they just weren't ready for sleep. Three of them lived in this little home in Springhill, PEI. The other two were on summer vacation with their parents from Maine. There was a whole houseful of adults at the dining room table. The grown-ups, some of them sisters and brothers, were truly enjoying their once-a-year visit with one another, just as the girls were. That, of course, was the reason the youngsters had been sent to bed early. It was time for the grown-ups to sit around the table, play 45's, get caught up on each other's lives … and tell stories. The girls were sitting quietly on the stairs, hoping they wouldn't be found out and sent back to bed before the stories started.

There was a door at the bottom of the stairs, but if you turned the doorknob very, very carefully, just when everyone was laughing at one of Uncle Frank's jokes, the grown-ups probably wouldn't hear it. Then you could leave the door open just a bit, just enough to hear what the adults were talking about.

It was at the home of Charlie and May Frost that this group of card players was assembled. Charlie's sister, Eva, was the mother of the two extra girls on the stairs. May's sister, Annie and her husband, Roland, were at the table as well. The girls were well aware that Uncle Roland was the best story-teller in the world, maybe even in all of PEI! They had no intention of being sent back to bed. They did not want to miss hearing Uncle Roland's stories!

The door was open just a crack, but the house was small and the men's voices became louder as the glasses got filled up for the second time. The girls waited patiently through the first round of cards, while the talk was about what was new since the American sisters had visited last summer. They waited through the second round of cards, while the talk was of old friends from their childhood and of how the elderly of their own families were faring. After the third round, May got up to get sandwiches ready and put the kettle on. The girls stifled their giggles, their hands over their mouths, terrified that they would be discovered and sent back up to bed. The talk at the table had now turned to old times, escapades from their youth, characters from the community, past and present. This was getting interesting! There were funny stories about their parents' childhood, stories of unsolved mysteries from years past, reminders of tricks they had played on one another in the long ago.

Then someone mentioned the Burning Ship. "You saw it pretty close up one time, didn't you, Roland?" On the stairs, as around the table, a quietness settled. Roland began to speak.

"It was a warm evening in the fall of the year. I'd gone out for a smoke and a walk along the shore. It was a quiet night, not much wind blowing. Peaceful! After a bit I saw a light on the water. I couldn't figure out what it might be. I got down close to the shore and I could see it was a sailing ship, with high masts and full sails. It seemed awfully close to shore. I couldn't think where it could have come from. All of a sudden, as I was standing there watching, it burst into flames! The sails were burning and the deck was on fire! I could see people running around back and forth, some of them jumping into the water. I ran to my dory, scared I wouldn't get out there on time to help them. I rowed as hard as I could towards them, but the ship was sinking. It sank right in front of my eyes. The masts collapsed into the water. And it was just … gone. Like it had never been there. No waves rolling in to shore. No flames on the water. There was nothing left of it! That's when I realized that I had never heard a sound. No fire crackling, no yelling from the people on deck, no wind roaring, nothing! By the time I got back to shore I knew for sure that I had seen the Burning Ship. I've seen it once or twice since, but it was never like that time."

For a few minutes no one spoke. The girls crept back up the stairs and snuggled down in their beds. They could hear the conversation resuming around the table. Their minds were filled with wonder. What was it that Uncle Roland had seen? How could a big ship like that burn and disappear into the water without anyone else seeing it? What happened to the people on it?

As adults, the girls tried to satisfy their curiosity by reading everything they could about the phenomenon that was the Burning Ship. They read the scientific explanations and the supernatural ones. None of it made sense to them. Always they remembered Roland's story and the fear and amazement they had felt while they listened. They knew Roland had seen what he said he had seen. But why? How? Sometimes they talked about it when they got together, remembering the night they crept down the stairs to hear a great story-teller give them the story that stayed with them for a lifetime.

THE CLOCK AND THE CHEST

Two cherished family heirlooms have a place in the home of this writer. One of them is a large chest made of pine. On the inside of the lid is this inscription, written in pencil: "I filled this box 9 May, 1922." Then the initials: N McL. The N was printed backwards. On the outside of the lid, the initials are carved into the wood in the same way, with the N carved backwards. The chest belonged to my great-grandfather, Norman MacLennan. It was this chest he filled with clothing and other worldly goods when he travelled to British Columbia for the second time. He had hoped to make a good living there with his skill as a sawyer. His intention was to spend the rest of his life in British

Columbia, working in the lumber industry. That plan did not work out for him. The industry had changed when new kinds of machinery became available to lumber companies. The skills that had kept sawyers like Norman in demand for so many years were no longer required.

When Norman returned to Prince Edward Island from this second trip to British Columbia he was a tired, discouraged old man, with no money and no home. He had sold his farm to get the money to make the second trip west. Even that wasn't enough, as he had to borrow to get train passage for himself and Sophie.

I discovered a smaller wooden chest in the basement of my husband's ancestral home in Tyne Valley, where we have lived since moving back to Prince Edward Island to his family's farm. I had gone down to put wood in the furnace and I noticed the chest tucked into a dark corner. It had the same inscription on the lid as the one on the chest my mother had given me, which now had a new life in our home as a toy box for our children. My mother explained to me that my great-grandfather, Norman, had borrowed money from my husband's great-grandfather, Dan MacLean, to pay for his passage west the second time. When he returned he was destitute and had no way to repay his debts. He offered his chest of tools as repayment for the loan. Thus it was that the chest which had belonged to my great-grandfather came to be found in my husband's family home.

When my mother and father retired, they bought a smaller home and didn't have room for everything from the farmhouse. They gave me a mantle clock, which had been a wedding gift to them from my mother's Aunt Druscilla Congdon.

Charlie Frost left home as a young man to make

a living. According to Island tradition, his younger brother would inherit the family farm. Charlie had an adventurous spirit and since his older sisters had already gone to work in the United States, he decided to try his hand at finding work there as well. He did find work, as he was willing to do whatever would pay him a wage. He began by helping to dig the subway in New York City. There were areas that had to be dug by hand. It was back-breaking labour and difficult to find men who were willing to do it, but he stayed with it until he found another job. His next job was painting and hanging wall paper. Eventually he went to work for his brother-in-law, who owned a gas station in Portland, Maine.

May Enman was a teacher. There were lots of positions available for teachers on Prince Edward Island, so she had her choice of schools. A new teacher created quite a sensation in a community, especially among the young men of the area. May was invited to dances and house parties, church picnics and meetings. She met more than one young man who would have liked a serious relationship with her. However, May's heart was not really free. She cared deeply for Charlie, but she didn't know if he felt the same way towards her or if he valued her only as a friend. They had grown up together on the Enmore Road and their families had been close friends. It was not unusual for old friends to correspond, especially when one of them was far from home. She decided to write to Charlie to keep him updated on the lives of their friends and on activities in Enmore. All of his sisters had moved to the United States, so there was no one to give him the news of the young people of Enmore. She also had lots of stories to tell him about the shenanigans of her students. She was pleased that he always answered her letters.

May was teaching in Chelton and boarding with a woman and her two adult children. The daughter and son were both close to May's age. She and the daughter became very close friends. The son very much wanted a steady relationship with May, but she always put him off, saying she was not interested in anything serious. When she would go to community events with her friend, the brother would always insist on escorting them. She tried not to hurt his feelings but she made it clear to him that they could be friends and nothing more.

For a couple of months she heard nothing from Charlie and she was beginning to believe that he had met someone in whom he was seriously interested. One day she and her girlfriend were out for a walk and she confided that she had not heard from Charlie in a long time. The look on her friend's face spoke volumes. Immediately, her friend led her to a large rock beside the lane. Under the rock were letters from Charlie, written over a period of many weeks. "My brother knew who his competition was," her friend said. "I just found out yesterday what he was doing, when I saw him coming from the mailbox. He stopped in the lane and put something under this rock. I thought I knew what it might be, but I came out and checked when he wasn't home. I was waiting for a chance to tell you."

May found a new boarding house very soon, using the excuse to her landlady that it was a much shorter walk to the school.

That July, Aunt Druscilla Congdon made her usual visit to the Enman farm while May was home on summer holidays. Aunt Dru, Toff's older sister, had married into wealth in Maine and she wanted to see her niece do "better" in life than being "just a country school teacher." Dru's daughter, Isabel, was looking for a nanny for her children as she had a very active social life and was often expected to entertain her husband's business associates. Dru was hopeful that she might connect May with some well-to-do young man who would be worthy of her and offer her an easier life than the one she would have as a country school teacher.

May wasn't as hard to convince as Dru expected. Although she hated to disappoint her father, who had worked so hard to send her to Teacher's College, May was excited about this opportunity. She told her father that she wouldn't stay long, perhaps for a year. Prince Edward Island was her home and she loved teaching, but the chance to experience city life for a short time seemed like an adventure not to be missed. She told no one about her other reason for wanting to go to the States, because she had no idea if anything would come of it.

At first, May really enjoyed her time in Maine. She was fond of Isabel's children, but felt sorry that their mother seemed to have so little time for them as she rushed around to teas and committee meetings. May had one half-day to herself each week and she soon learned to enjoy this time. Sometimes she visited the Frost girls who were living in Maine. She learned to take the bus to Jessie's house. Jessie was newly married and no longer working. Eva and Anna were at work during the day and Marjorie had moved to New York.

On one of her afternoons off, May decided to go to a movie, an exciting 'city' thing to do. The theatre was almost empty so she sat in a row of seats all by herself. She glanced up as the movie was just about to start and noticed a tall, dark-haired man come in to the same row where she was sitting. She expected him to go to the far end of the row, but he came and sat right beside her. She kept her head down, trying to ignore him. Then a familiar voice asked, "Aren't you going to say hello, May?" She looked up, startled, and there was Charlie!

Charlie had a few days off and had decided to spend them with his sisters. When he got to Jessie's house she told him where to find May. From then on they spent every possible minute together. Before that visit was over, they had both decided that city life was not for them. Early that summer Charlie took May and Anna home to Prince Edward Island. That was the beginning of Charlie and May's courtship. It was a great summer of horse races, dances, ball games, and lots of fun. In September of 1933, they were married on the Island they loved and would call home for the rest of their lives.

Aunt Dru had done her best to stop the courtship between May and Charlie. This was certainly not what she had intended when she convinced May to come to Maine. Dru reminded May that these were hard times, the 'Dirty Thirties.' She told May repeatedly, "When poverty comes in the door, love goes out the window." She was sure this relationship would be a disaster for her niece. However, when she realized that there was nothing she could do to stop the marriage, she gave them a wedding gift. It was a mantle clock that chimed the hours.

Several years later, Dru came to visit May and Charlie in their little farmhouse in Springhill. There were three or four children by then and yes, there was certainly poverty by Aunt Dru's standards. But that little house was filled with love and May was happier than Dru had ever seen her. The clock she had given them sat proudly on a shelf that Charlie had made for it. Before her visit was over, she took May aside and said, "I was wrong, May. You made the best choice."

The clock is a symbol of a love that lasted for a

lifetime, through good times and bad, disagreements and laughter. Nine children were brought up believing that love is better than anything money can buy, dancing beats crying every time, and when times get really tough the best thing to do is look your troubles in the face and ask God for help to show you the way.

GENEALOGY OF THE FROST FAMILY OF ENMORE

1. John Ellis Frost of Wales married Grace Baglole of PEI.

2. Thomas Charles Frost, b. March 7, 1853, d. 1936, married Margaret Rogers Murray, b. 1847, d. 1909.

3. Alfred Long Frost, b. 1883, d. 1966, married Christy Ann MacLeod, b. May 6, 1881, d. January 27, 1965. Children: Marjorie, Jessie, Charlie, Eva, Anna, Lloyd.

4. Charles Thomas Frost, b. July 30, 1908, d. July 18, 1986, married May Lillian Enman, b. November 14, 1907, d. April 24, 1999.

GENEALOGY OF THE ENMAN FAMILY OF ENMORE

1. Jeremiah Enman of Ireland married Margaret Benoit of USA, died as a Loyalist, emigrated to Vernon River, PEI, during the American Revolution after her husband's death.

2. Thomas Enman, b. New York, 1780, d. 1887, married Snazelle Sawtelle, b. Scotland, 1787, d. 1864.

3. David Enman, b. 1810, d. 1893, married Abigail Wood, b. 1814, d. 1897.

4. Theophilus Enman (Offie), b. 1834, d. 1917, married Johanna Young, b. 1835, d. 1915.

5. Theophilus Enman (Toff), b. 1881, d. 1956, married Eliza MacLennan, b. 1883, d. 1977.

6. May Enman, b. 1907, d. 1999, married Charles Frost, 1908-1986.